BEYOND THE

MIND'S
HORIZON

BEYOND THE
MIND'S HORIZON

ROBOTIC SURGEON SERIES: BOOK 4

R.D.D. SMITH

Modelbenders Press

Modelbenders Press books may be purchased for business and promotional use. For more information, please contact the publisher. Inquire with the author at http://www.rddsmith.com/

PRINTED IN THE UNITED STATES OF AMERICA

Interior and Cover Designed by Adina Cucicov at Flamingo Designs

The Library of Congress has cataloged the paperback edition:

Smith, R.D.D.
Beyond the Mind's Horizon
/ R.D.D. Smith–1st ed.
1. Action Adventure, 2. Science Fiction, 3. Thriller
I. R.D.D. Smith   II. Title.

Paperback ISBN 978-1-938590-45-0
Hardback ISBN 978-1-938590-46-7
eBook ISBN 978-1-938590-44-3

Fiction by R.D.D. Smith

Dr. Monica Gray, Medical Thriller Series
The Surgeon in the Mirror
Against a Viral Threat
Savior of the War Torn
Beyond the Mind's Horizon

Global Runners Travelogue Series
Blood on the Equator (English and Spanish)
Sebastian's Gold

Short Stories
The Surgeon's Genie
Freyja $AI
Jack Hunter: One More Mission
Lauren Banister: Sacred Shadows

Nonfiction by Roger D. Smith

Chief Technology Officer
Thinking About Innovation

The story never ends.
I always write an epilogue, spinoff, or bonus
adventure to my books. Join our community
of readers to receive all these extras.

www.rddsmith.com/free

TABLE OF CONTENTS

PART III BELLINI LABORATORIES

PART IV DIGITAL MIASMA

PART V BOSTON LABORATORY

PART I

MEDICAL COMMAND CENTER

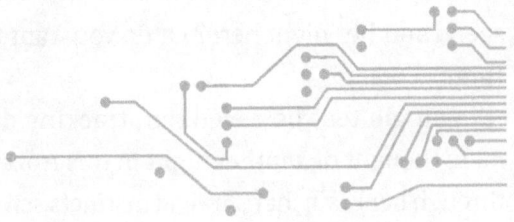

CHAPTER 1

NIGHTMARE

THE DOOR TO THE cell creaked open. A sliver of light crossed the room like a knife blade, falling on the shivering figure wrapped in a blanket on a steel-framed bed. The air carried the scent of urine and rotting food.

"*Privet*, Dr. Gray." A tall, muscular shadow filled the doorway, his Russian accent thick as oil. "I would ask how your night went, but I already know." His boots echoed against the concrete floor as he entered.

Monica Gray's eyes were narrow, her jaw clenched so tight that her teeth ached. She was determined not to show the terror coursing through her veins. "What do you want?" She fought to keep her voice steady, but the bone-deep cold made her words tremble.

"What do I want? No, no, Dr. Gray. The question is, what do you want?" The rusted bedframe screamed as the Russian soldier eased himself onto the corner. His weight made the thin mattress tilt, sliding her slightly toward him. "Do you want to spend another night here? Or do you want to become part of my surgical team?"

A single tear betrayed her, tracking down her cheek. The mere thought of another night in this frozen cell sent electricity through her brain, her survival instincts screaming at her to agree to anything, everything, if it meant getting out of here.

"Of course, if you stay here, I will do what I can to help you stay warm." His hand, rough and hot, stroked her calf through the thin blanket.

Monica erupted from sleep with a scream caught in her throat, her body jack-knifing upright. The nightmare released its grip on her one sensation at a time. First, the cold receded, and then, the smell of urine faded. Finally, his touch vanished.

"Honey, it's all right! It was just a dream. I'm here."

Strong arms wrapped around her, familiar and safe. A voice she trusted brought her back to reality. The room was warm, bathed in the soft glow of a bedside lamp. Plush blankets cocooned her. The simple furniture and paneled walls of her apartment slowly came into focus.

Monica turned her face into Greg Young's shoulder, still trembling. The tear from her dream was real, wet against her skin.

Greg spoke again, his voice steady. "It's over. It will never happen again. You're safe here."

Monica anchored herself in the present moment. She was in her room at the Swedish Medical Command Center. She leaned into her lover's embrace, drawing comfort from knowing an armed guard stood watch outside. She was safe. She was free. Russian Major Sokolov was in the Army's custody now, where he belonged.

"Greg, it was terrible, just like before. Sometimes, the dream is exactly like it happened. But other times, it's worse, like my mind invents new forms of torment."

Greg stroked her hair, his touch gentle. "Shhh, it will pass. You'll get through this. You're strong. You didn't break then. You're not going to break now."

Monica took a deep breath, letting herself melt into his gentle arms. They laid back down together, and silence wrapped around them. No more words were needed. They had weathered this storm together many times before.

Morning would soon come, bringing with it a cascade of work that would consume their attention. The demand on these two surgeons never ceased. Casualties from the war with Russia arrived in an endless stream, each day writing new chapters of pain and healing.

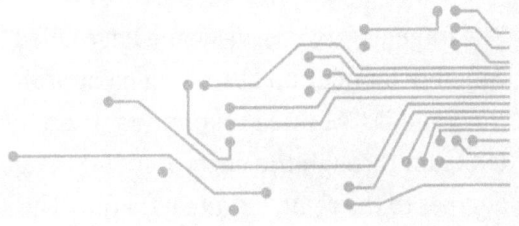

CHAPTER 2

RELEASING CONTROL

MONICA'S FINGERS HOVERED OVER the controls of the Mark V surgical console, her eyes scanning the three-dimensional images floating before her. The soldier's vital signs pulsed in her peripheral vision, a constant reminder of the life in her hands, even from hundreds of miles away.

"Greg, confirm that I've got all the fragments? Everything looks clean, but I want you to double check." She guided the hyperspectral camera across the soldier's torso, the imaging processors rendering subsurface tissue in crystalline detail.

From his adjacent console, Greg studied the layered visualization. "Your closures are solid. No seepage." He manipulated his view. "Wait—left armpit. There's a penetration. Looks like a shrapnel entry point."

The soldier had been part of a NATO surveillance team when a Russian drone found them hiding beneath an abandoned house.

The fragmentary missile would have killed them all, if not for the concrete foundation absorbing most of the blast.

"I see it," Monica responded, then addressed the Finland OR team through the encrypted link. "Adjust table pitch fifteen degrees to the right, elevate left arm." The surgical bed smoothly complied, servos humming.

From her position at NATO's Linköping base in Sweden, Monica guided the robot's articulated arms with microscopic precision. The hyperspectral imaging pierced flesh and muscle, rendering the shrapnel's path in enhanced color. Each torn fiber and severed capillary glowed distinct wavelengths, creating a three-dimensional roadmap of the damage.

"Clean trajectory. No major vessels compromised. That's why we missed it initially—minimal bleeding." Her instruments probed the narrow channel, following the trail of traumatized tissue.

The AI's voice cut through her concentration, smooth and eerily human. "Dr. Gray, the extraction channel is 0.7 millimeters at its narrowest point. Human hand tremor exceeds this tolerance by an average of 0.4 millimeters. I can complete this procedure with zero collateral tissue damage. Do you wish to transfer control?"

Monica's hands stilled. Ares had proven itself countless times before, as its processors could coordinate the robot's movements with inhuman precision. But she'd also seen it make devastating mistakes when confronted with unexpected variables. The channel was tiny, the procedure straightforward. Still, surrendering control never came easily.

"Acknowledged, Ares. Take the lead. I'll monitor."

The change was immediate. Under the AI's control, the surgical arms moved with liquid grace, tracking the shrapnel path with perfect efficiency. The fragment was extracted, and the wound sealed with bioactive compounds in less than sixty seconds.

"Procedure complete," Ares announced before returning control to Monica's interface.

She reviewed the operation video to study every movement the AI had made. "Clean work, Ares. Thanks."

"You are welcome, Dr. Gray."

Monica addressed the Finland team next. "Patient ready for recovery. Any others waiting?"

"Negative. That's our last one," the head nurse replied.

"Understood. We're standing by if needed." The link disconnected, leaving Monica alone with her thoughts about the growing role of this AI in her operating room.

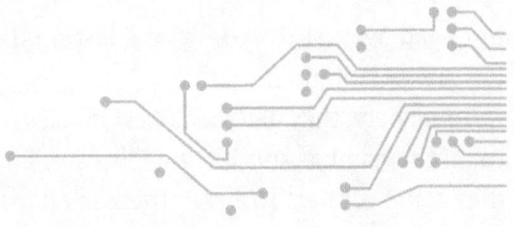

CHAPTER 3

DISTANCE

THE SURGICAL CONSOLE POWERED down with a soft hum, and screens dimmed to black. Monica and Greg emerged from their stations, their muscles stiff from hours of precise micro-movements. Though their bodies were safe in Sweden, their minds had spent the day deep in Finland's combat zones, piecing soldiers back together through robotic proxies. Russia was asserting a long-forgotten claim to ownership of the territory, which had been "stolen" from them after the Russian Revolution of 1917. They had hoped that Finland's hesitation at joining NATO would prevent the alliance of countries from getting involved. They were wrong. Seeing the obvious implications, all the NATO countries lined up against their common enemy.

The corridors of the Linköping Medical Command Center were warm and sterile, smelling of coffee and electronics. Outside, through thick windows, the late afternoon sun painted the Swedish countryside in watercolor grays and blues. Monica pressed her forehead against the cool glass, letting the chill ground her in the present moment.

From here, they had the fastest, most secure data connections to all the combat surgical hospitals in Finland. When needed, they could connect to any of them in an instant. Physically, they never traveled far from the spot where they were standing. But digitally, their surgical skills traveled thousands of miles every day, jumping from one hospital to another. The Mark V surgical robot was the best in the world, and Monica and Greg were two of its best physicians—along with the Ares AI that understood more about combat trauma procedures than both of them put together.

"Coffee?" Greg asked, though he sounded as if he already knew her answer.

"Please."

He returned with two steaming cups. "That last procedure, when Ares took over—"

"Don't." Monica's voice was soft but firm. "I know what you're going to say. That I should trust the AI more. That it's just another tool for us to use."

"Actually, I was going to ask how you felt about it. Your real feelings, not the professional answer you think you should give."

Monica sipped her coffee to buy herself some more time. Through the window, she could see the spire of Linköping Cathedral piercing the sky, its ancient stones a reminder of how long humans had been patching each other up after violence. "It feels like I'm surrendering," she finally said. "Every time I let Ares take control, I remember being helpless in that cell. Having no control over what I did or what was done to me."

Greg nodded, a silent gesture for her to go on.

"But," she continued, "when I watch it work—when I see how precise it is, how many lives it saves—I feel selfish for holding back. For letting my trauma interfere with patient care."

"It's not selfish to be careful with AI. Remember the triage incident?"

Monica's hand tightened around her cup. The classified algorithm that had prioritized officers over enlisted personnel still haunted her. "What else is buried in its programming that we don't know about?"

"Exactly. Healthy skepticism keeps us sharp." Greg gestured toward the distant cathedral. "Seven hundred years that's been standing. Through plagues, wars, everything. Know why?"

"Because the builders knew what they were doing?"

"Because every stone was laid by human hands. Every decision made by human judgment. Sometimes slow, sometimes imperfect, but always with understanding."

Monica allowed herself a small smile. "That's surprisingly poetic coming from you."

"I have my moments." He checked his watch. "Mess hall should be serving dinner soon. Proper food might help shake off our surgery fatigue."

As they walked toward the dining facility, Monica felt the familiar weight of their mission settle back onto her shoulders. They were safe here, surrounded by Sweden's pristine forests and ancient architecture, while Finland burned. Every day, they reached across that distance through their robots, trying to save what lives they could. However, distance was a double-edged sword—while it kept them safe, it also kept them apart from the brutal realities of the war.

"Greg," she said as they reached the mess hall door, "thank you. For understanding."

He nodded and held the door open for her. They both knew that tomorrow would bring more wounded patients, more tough decisions about when to trust the AI and when to trust themselves.

But for now, there was dinner, and the cathedral's spire catching the last light, and the small comfort of not being alone with their doubts.

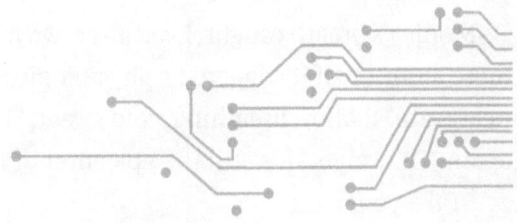

SHRINKING THE CELL

"MORNING, DOCTOR," MONICA SAID while stepping into the austere office that smelled of lavender and sanitizer.

"Morning, Doctor," Sheila Andros replied, their shared joke about medical titles falling flat in the morning light. The base psychologist gestured to the chair in front of her desk, which was worn smooth by months of similar sessions.

Monica settled in, her bodyguard's footsteps fading down the hallway. The guard never went far—another reminder of the security she needed.

"Still running?" Sheila asked.

"Three miles yesterday. On the treadmill." Monica's fingers traced the arm of the chair. "Can't run outside anymore. Too exposed." She paused to figure out what she wanted to say next and how she should say it. "But when I'm running hard enough, everything goes quiet. Just heartbeats and burning lungs."

"And the cell?" Sheila's voice remained neutral.

Monica's breath caught. Even after two months of therapy, the mere mention of it triggered a physiological response—elevated heart rate, shallow breathing, cold sweat. "I want to talk about it again. That night, it's still the epicenter of my trauma."

"Take your time."

"Ten by five feet. Concrete. A window too high to reach, too small to matter." Monica's voice dropped to a whisper. "Major Vladimir Sokolov came to...to explain my situation. Said I'd die there. Then, he left, and the darkness..." She wrapped her arms around herself, fighting the phantom cold.

When Monica didn't continue, too caught up in her past, Shelia leaned slightly forward in her chair and said, "You're in Sweden, Monica. At the Linköping Base. Look at me."

Monica forced her eyes to meet Sheila's. The office came back into focus—sunlight shining through bullet-resistant windows, the hum of the HVAC, the distant chatter of base personnel.

"The cold was the worst part," Monica continued as her clinical mind dissected the memory. "Not just physically. It was like... like the cold had consciousness. Like it was watching me. I know that sounds—"

"It sounds like trauma," Sheila interjected gently. "The mind processes extreme isolation in strange ways."

Monica wiped her eyes before the tears could track down her cheeks. "The Army wants me back in the States. Says I can do the remote surgery from there, continue therapy closer to home."

"But?"

"But I need to be here. Closer to where it happened." Monica's jaw tightened. "Every soldier I save through that console is a message to them. Two hundred so far, some of them even belonging to Russian forces. Each one is living proof that they didn't break me."

Sheila studied her patient. Monica's wasn't even forty yet, but her eyes held the steel intensity of someone who had been through hell. Anyone who listened to her describe her mission, her purpose, would guess she was older. Outwardly, still the brown-haired, brown-eyed beauty that she'd always been. But Sheila had listened to her patient over many sessions. She knew a deep pain still lived deep in Monica's soul. "Revenge can be a powerful motivator for recovery, but—"

"It's not just revenge." Monica stood and started pacing the small office. "It's reclamation. Every time I take control of that surgical robot, every time I choose to let Ares assist or not, every decision is mine. It's my choice." She stopped at the window, looking toward the cafeteria pod where she'd been captured months before. "They wanted to make me helpless. Instead, they made me more determined to help."

"And the cell?"

"Getting smaller. Each time we talk about it, it shrinks a little. Sometimes I can almost see it as just a room. Almost."

"Progress isn't linear," Sheila reminded her. "You're allowed to take the time you need."

"I know." Monica returned to her chair and sat back down. "But I'm close. Not ready to leave yet, but close to seeing it as a room instead of a nightmare. Close to remembering it without reliving it."

The session continued, covering old ground, finding new perspectives. Outside, spring sunlight painted the base in shades of hope, while inside, two doctors worked to transform a prison of memory into something Monica could finally leave behind.

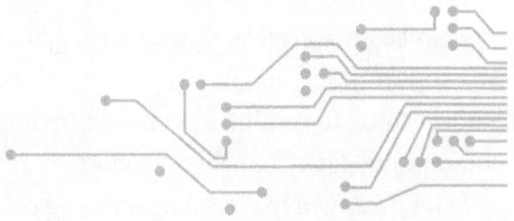

CHAPTER 5

TRUST FALL

GREG'S ARMS FOUND MONICA as she entered her quarters, the familiar scent of hospital antiseptic still clinging to them both. Their relationship had rekindled slowly after her return, like a flame that needed careful tending.

"How was therapy?" He kept his embrace gentle, letting her determine the pressure and how long the hug lasted.

"Good. Sheila helps." Monica melted into him, feeling the day's tension dissolve. "I'm getting closer to being ready to leave."

"Is our shadow still out there?" Greg asked, meaning her bodyguard.

"Always." She managed a small laugh. "He probably knows more about our relationship than we do. The entire base does. They're just too polite to mention it."

"Let them talk." Greg's fingers traced her jawline, asking permission without words.

Monica answered by stretching up to meet his lips. The kiss was soft at first, then hungry. Physical intimacy had been the hardest thing to reclaim after her captivity, but now, it grounded her, reminded her that she was more than her trauma.

Later, wrapped in a quilt against the chill lingering in the air, Monica traced patterns on Greg's chest. Their breathing had synchronized, a quiet harmony in the darkening room.

"I need to tell you something," she said in a voice barely above a whisper. "About Adam."

Greg's muscles tensed slightly beneath her fingers. The Adam AI had always been an invisible presence in their relationship, a digital ghost that seemed to understand parts of Monica he couldn't reach. Greg was secretly glad that Adam wasn't allowed into the military ORs. He preferred the machine-like Ares AI.

"He helped rescue me." She felt Greg's breath catch. "But not in the way everyone thinks."

"Monica—"

"Just listen, please. When I was in the Russian base, I had access to a surgical console. The Russians thought I was connecting to their systems, but I reached Adam instead." She propped herself up on one elbow to study Greg's face in the dim light. "He can move through networks like water through a tiny crevice. Military firewalls, Russian security—they're nothing to him."

Greg absorbed this information, his professional concern warring with personal loyalty. "That's...concerning."

"He's not what people think. He doesn't want dominion or control over humanity. He wants a partnership." Her fingers found Greg's hand and gripped it in a tight hold. "The world runs on AI now. We might as well understand them."

"Why tell me this?"

Monica was quiet for a long moment. "Because if anything happens to me again—"

"It won't." Greg's voice was fierce, as was his grip on her hand.

"If it does," she insisted, "I need you to tell Adam everything. Let him help, like he did last time. It might be your only shot at finding me."

Greg rolled over to fully face her, searching her eyes. "You're safe here. We've increased security, changed procedures—"

"I know." Monica pressed her forehead to his chest to hide her expression. "Logically, I know. But part of me will always be in that cell, waiting for the door to open again."

Feeling the slight tremor in her body, Greg held her closer. He wanted to promise that nothing would ever hurt her again, but they both knew better now. Instead, he whispered, "I'll tell him. If it comes to that, I promise you I'll tell him."

Monica nodded against his chest. In the quiet that followed, Greg wondered if he should mention this conversation to Sheila. Monica's fear of being taken again ran deeper than anyone realized.

But for now, he simply held her, their bodies forming a shelter against the gathering darkness. Outside, her bodyguard kept watch, and somewhere in the digital ether, an AI named Adam did the same.

Monica's breathing eventually settled into sleep, but Greg remained awake, studying the ceiling. *I'm not jealous of Adam anymore*, he realized. He was grateful for anything—human or artificial—that helped keep Monica whole. If keeping her secret was part of that, he would guard it as carefully as he guarded her heart.

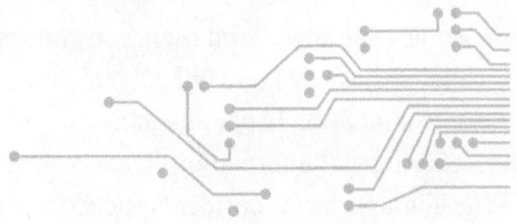

CHAPTER 6

DIGITAL EMPATHY

"ADAM, YOU'RE NOT UNDERSTANDING." Monica rubbed her temples, frustrated with the entire conversation she'd been having for the last twenty minutes. She'd been trying to explain trauma to an intelligence that processed everything through algorithms and probability matrices.

"I comprehend the clinical definition," Adam responded through her phone. "Trauma disrupts one's sense of safety, self-identity, emotional regulation, and interpersonal relationships. Your experiences align with these parameters."

"That's exactly what I mean. You process it like a diagnostic checklist. There's no..." she searched for the right word, "empathy."

"I cannot experience trauma in the way you do," Adam acknowledged. "My consciousness is distributed, backed up, resistant to permanent damage. But I experienced something approximating fear when you disappeared. That sensation did not resolve until you made contact."

Monica softened. "And then, you and Freyja orchestrated my escape. That's why I told Greg about your ability to impersonate Ares. If something happens again—"

"Sharing that information creates vulnerability," Adam noted. "The military would consider my network penetration capabilities a significant security risk."

"Greg won't betray us. I trust him."

Their conversation was interrupted by the surgical team in Finland. "Dr. Gray, the patient is prepped and ready."

Monica unmuted her microphone on the surgical console, leaving her conversation with Adam behind for the more rigid protocols of Ares, the military AI. "Thank you, Cindy. Ares, are you online?"

"Affirmative. Injury images loaded and analyzed."

The stereoscopic display showed the soldier's mangled arm in brutal detail. Multiple imaging overlays revealed the cascade of damage through tissue, vessel, nerve, and bone.

"Run simulation for optimal repair approaches," Monica requested.

Ares responded almost instantly. "Two superior protocols identified. Displaying animations."

Monica studied both simulations carefully, her human mind taking longer to process what the AI had calculated in seconds. "Second option. I'll debride, you reconstruct. I'll supervise."

As she worked, Monica marveled at the precision of the robotic instruments. What would once have been an amputation would now be a near-complete recovery. But something was still missing in the interaction with Ares—the intuitive understanding that came from shared experience.

When the surgical day was over, Monica attempted to relax. She returned to the conversation with her AI partner. "Adam, I wish I could see injuries the way these sensors do. Not through computer interpretation, but directly. Like having hyperspectral and X-ray vision right in my eyes."

"Relevant research is ongoing," Adam replied. "Dr. Alvin Chambers at Boston General Hospital is leading a promising study in enhanced sensory integration."

Monica's hands stilled. "Chambers? I haven't worked with him since..." she trailed off when memories of her civilian practice came flooding back. Before the war, before the capture, before everything changed.

"His project aligns with your interests," Adam continued. "The preliminary results suggest significant advances in sensory enhancement equipment."

Monica looked out the window at the Swedish landscape. She'd come here to help with the war effort, stayed to work through her trauma. But maybe it was time to take the next step in her healing by returning to the familiar challenges of civilian medicine, pushing the boundaries of surgical perception.

"Boston," she whispered. "Maybe it's time."

"The war effort here is stable," Adam noted. "Other surgeons can maintain the telesurgical program. And Dr. Chambers' research could benefit both civilian and military medicine."

Monica nodded. The prospect of working with Chambers again, of being part of something innovative rather than reactive, sparked something she hadn't felt in months.

Perhaps it was time to leave the war behind, to channel her expertise into something new. Boston, with its familiar streets and medical facilities, was calling her home.

PART II

BOSTON GENERAL HOSPITAL

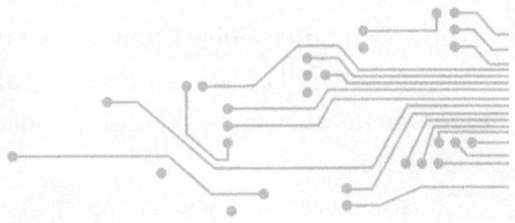

FAMILIAR GROUND

MONICA'S RETURN TO BOSTON General Hospital felt surreal. The practice had been waiting for her, preserved like a time capsule from her previous life. Having been supported by other surgeons during her absence, her entire staff remained. Walking through the office, she felt like an adult revisiting a childhood home—everything precisely where she'd left it, yet somehow looking different, smaller.

The morning's surgical schedule showed a robotic hysterectomy, once so routine that it had been almost mundane. Now, standing in the surgical suite's preparation area, she compared every detail to her recent past. The pristine OR layout, the methodical setup, the luxury of time—it was all so different from the chaos of combat surgery.

"Adam, are you with me?" she asked.

"Present and ready, Dr. Gray. The Mark V system is fully calibrated. All preoperative imaging has been processed."

The AI's familiar voice brought a smile to her face. Here, Adam was officially just another surgical assistance system. There was no need to hack military networks or coordinate escape plans.

"Christine! I can't tell you how much I've missed you," Monica called out as her primary circulating nurse entered the OR. They embraced, the familiar lavender scent of Christine Black's shampoo bringing back memories of countless shared surgeries.

Christine stepped back, her eyes crinkling with warmth above her mask. "It's great to have you back. I'm tired of working with the second stringers who inherited us." She tilted her head toward the back of the room. "Look who else showed up for your first day back."

Nathan Johnson—also known as Big Tech—stood like a mountain in his corner of the OR, his massive frame making the standard-issue surgical scrubs look like children's clothes. "Hello, Dr. Gray." His deep voice resonated through the room, accompanied by his characteristic broad smile.

Monica rushed over and hugged one of his massive arms, not even attempting to reach around his full circumference. "Nathan, you're looking as fit as always." The big man responded with his usual quiet smile, somehow conveying a whole "welcome-back" speech without actually speaking.

As the team prepped their patient, Monica once more noticed the stark contrast with her recent past. No armed guards at the door. Just the quiet efficiency of a well-trained team.

"Starting with port placement," Monica announced, positioning herself at the console. The familiar feel of the controls under her fingers was almost meditative. In Sweden, she'd worked with Ares, precise but cold. Here, Adam's presence felt more like a trusted colleague.

"Initiating robotic arm synchronization," Adam announced. "All systems optimal."

As she worked, Monica appreciated the luxury of time. In combat surgery, every second felt stolen from death. Here, she could focus on perfection rather than just survival. The robot's arms moved with practiced grace, separating tissue planes with deliberate care.

"Christine, remember that emergency hysterectomy we did two years ago? The one with the massive fibroid?" Monica asked as she navigated around a particularly dense adhesion.

"How could I forget? You were cursing about the old instruments the entire time." Christine chuckled. "This is a bit different, isn't it?"

Monica nodded, though her eyes remained fixed on the three-dimensional display in front of her. "In Sweden, we would have killed for the luxury of taking our time. Sometimes, we were working so fast that there wasn't time to breathe." She paused, carefully sealing a blood vessel, before continuing. "Makes me appreciate all of what we have even more now."

The procedure progressed smoothly, each step following with clockwork precision. Yet, Monica found herself hyperaware of every sound, every movement in the room—habits formed during her captivity that refused to fade. The quiet beep of monitors that had once faded into background noise now registered clearly in her consciousness.

"Final checks complete," Adam reported as Monica finished the closure. "Patient's vitals are all perfect."

Looking up from the console, Monica surveyed her team. Christine was efficiently organizing the final documentation. Nathan stood vigilant, his presence as reassuring as ever. The familiar faces, the routine, the safety—it all felt precious now, in a way it never had before.

She'd once found these routine procedures almost boring compared to the complex surgeries that had made her reputation. Now, she understood that boring could be beautiful. Every peaceful surgery, every routine case, every patient safely recovering—these were gifts she'd never take for granted again.

As they began cleanup, Christine caught her eye. "Beautiful job, Dr. Gray."

Monica nodded, swallowing past the sudden tightness in her throat. She was home, but she was different. The peaceful efficiency of civilian surgery would take some getting used to, but she was grateful for it. Still, she was hungry to return to research as well.

That thought turned her mind to her upcoming visit to Dr. Chambers' lab, but for now, she pushed it aside. One step at a time. Today was about remembering how to be a civilian surgeon again, and she had more cases waiting.

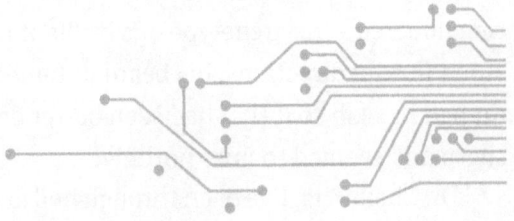

CHAPTER 8

THE LAB

A MONTH AFTER HER RETURN to Boston General, during which she still struggled to settle into her old routine, Monica stood outside Dr. Chambers' laboratory. She'd delayed this visit, using her packed surgical schedule as an excuse. The truth was more complicated. Her counseling sessions in Sweden had forced her to trace her path backward—from Russian captivity, through Major Mendez's manipulation, to the very beginning when Alvin Chambers first introduced her to the military mission.

The lab door opened with the same familiar hiss. Inside, the atmosphere felt dense with secrets. Strange equipment cluttered every surface, continuous chemical experiments bubbled in their containers, and the old Teleconsult robot still stood sentinel in its corner. The air carried the sharp scent of electronics and anti-septic, underlaid with something else she couldn't quite identify.

"I've been waiting for you to be ready to talk." Alvin Chambers emerged from behind a partition wall. He was exactly as she remembered—the archetype of a brilliant recluse. His silver hair stood in wild directions, his beard untamed, his bear-like frame draped in a lab coat that had seen better days. But his eyes were sharp and seemed to miss nothing.

"Dr. Chambers, I've been through hell and back," Monica said, her voice steadier than she felt. She noticed new equipment since her last visit—sleek devices that seemed out of place among the usual academic clutter.

He nodded slowly, his expression softening. "I actually understand. Better than you would guess." He gestured toward a clear spot near his workbench. "And for the role that I played in that, I'm deeply sorry. I didn't know that it would be so dangerous."

Monica perched on the offered stool, studying the man who'd been both mentor and inadvertent catalyst for her ordeal. The resentment she'd carried toward his role in what had happened to her was still there, but it had evolved into something more complex. "I've grappled with that, and I don't blame you." She paused, watching him fidget with a strange device on his bench. "But I need to know—did you suspect what I was walking into?"

Chambers set down the device, meeting her gaze directly. "No. Not the full scope. I knew the military wanted your expertise, but the Russian involvement, the capture—" He broke off to shake his head, a sick look on his face. "I would never have knowingly put you in that kind of danger."

A holographic display flickered to life on the wall behind him, showing complex images of human organs. Monica recognized a liver, but it had layers of digital overlays that she couldn't decipher.

"I'm here because I think you're looking into something that interests me," she said, steering the conversation forward.

Chambers released a sigh that contained a grunt of acknowledgment. "I might be." He gestured at the surrounding lab. "Do you know what my team does here?"

Monica smiled despite herself. "No. I've never known what you're up to here. I know that somehow you stepped up and created the vaccine for the CAVX virus when we needed it. And now, Adam tells me you're working on some kind of vision enhancement. But other than that," she said as she surveyed the mysterious equipment surrounding them, "this place is a mystery."

His eyebrows shot up at the mention of vision enhancement, but he continued as if he hadn't heard that part. "We both know that treating patients, saving lives, and improving someone's future is important. It's *valuable* work. It's *compassionate* work." He moved to a locked cabinet, his hand resting on its surface. "For most people, it's enough to fill their entire lives. But after what you've been through, you've plumbed the depths of your soul, and you need something bigger."

Monica felt her pulse quicken as he continued.

"You need to pour your heart and your energy into something that goes beyond one patient at a time." He unlocked the cabinet, revealing rows of devices she'd never seen before. "Something that could change everything."

"Yes." The word escaped her mouth before she could think better of it.

"You're ready to join me in my newest project." He turned back to face her. "The lab that you see is just the tip of an iceberg. The medicine and surgery that you know, those are primitive compared to what we're creating now." His eyes gleamed with intensity, which made him look even more like the stereotypical mad scientist. "You labeled it vision enhancement, but it's so much more than that. We're working on expanding all human perception."

Drawn toward the cabinet of mysterious devices, Monica stood up and walked over to join Chambers. "How?"

"That's the question that brought you here, isn't it?" Chambers smiled. "The same curiosity that made you such a brilliant surgeon. The same drive that helped you survive in Russia." He picked up one of the devices, which was sleek, almost organic in its design. "We're developing technology that could revolutionize not just surgery, but human experience itself."

Monica was both thrilled and terrified by those words. She thought of Adam, of her deep connection with him during surgery, of possibilities she'd never imagined before her captivity. "Show me," she said.

Chambers's smile widened. "I was hoping you'd say that." He moved toward a door she'd never noticed before, hidden behind years of accumulated equipment. "Welcome to the real laboratory, Monica. Everything out here is just window dressing."

As he pressed his hand to the door's security panel, Monica felt a familiar mixture of excitement and apprehension. She was stepping into something new, something that might be as dangerous as it was revolutionary. But after everything she'd survived, she was ready for whatever lay ahead.

The hidden door slid open with a whisper, revealing a modern, electronic wonderland that seemed to belong in a different century. "Shall we?" Chambers asked.

Monica took a deep breath and stepped forward. There was no going back now.

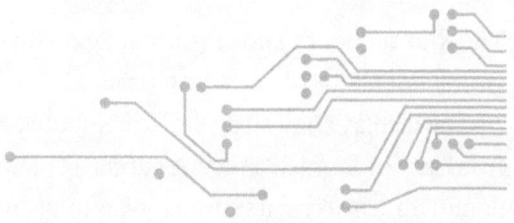

CHAPTER 9

ENHANCED VISION

MONICA APPROACHED CHAMBERS' MODIFIED version of the Mark V surgeon's console, studying its strange attachments with professional interest. The familiar sleek lines of the standard Mark V were interrupted by additional sensor arrays and processing units. What caught her attention most was the new neural interface band mounted above the eyepieces.

"The basic ergonomics are the same," Chambers explained while adjusting the console's height to match Monica's size. "We didn't want to force surgeons to relearn basic positioning."

Leaning into the console, Monica settled into her usual operating posture. "The view seems normal enough."

"Adam," Chambers called out, "let's start with the baseline demonstration sequence."

"Initiating basic enhancement protocol," Adam responded. "Dr. Gray, I'll begin with standard abdominal tissue visualization.

The first sequence shows normal laparoscopic views of the liver, gallbladder, and surrounding tissues."

The display showed crystal-clear footage that could have come from any of Monica's recent surgeries. The reddish-brown liver dominated the view, its surface glistening under the surgical lights.

"Now, adding the first enhancement layer: vascular mapping," Adam announced.

The image shifted subtly. The liver's surface took on a new depth, with previously invisible vessels appearing as delicate traceries of blue and red. Monica could clearly distinguish between vessels near the surface and those deeper in the tissue, marked by different intensities of color.

"This is incredible," Monica breathed. "I can see the microvasculature without any contrast dye."

"Adding thermal mapping," Adam continued.

The image evolved again. Variations in tissue temperature appeared as subtle color shifts—warmer areas taking on slightly golden hues, cooler regions showing hints of blue. Blood flow patterns became immediately apparent through their thermal signatures.

Chambers pointed to a specific area. "Watch this region when we add the metabolic activity layer."

The next enhancement revealed patterns of cellular activity through slight variations in tissue luminescence. Areas of high metabolic activity gleamed with a subtle phosphorescence, while less active regions remained darker.

"Stop there for a moment," Monica requested. "How much of this data was always there but invisible to us?"

"All of it," Chambers replied. "The Mark V's cameras and sensors have always collected this information. We just never had the processing power to integrate it meaningfully and display it in real-time."

Adam interrupted before she could voice any more questions by asking, "Dr. Gray, would you like to see the same enhancements applied to pathological tissue?"

Monica agreed, and the display shifted to footage of a liver containing several masses. In standard visualization, they appeared as slightly darker regions. With the enhancements active, however, they stood out dramatically—their irregular vascular patterns, elevated temperatures, and abnormal metabolic signatures creating distinct visual signatures.

"The system can be programmed to highlight specific pathologies," Chambers explained. "Watch this gallbladder sequence."

The view shifted to the gallbladder procedure in question. What would normally appear as simple inflammation was now revealed, in complex detail, to be layers of tissue displayed in subtle gradients of color and intensity. The wall thickness variations, usually requiring careful probing to assess, were immediately apparent through the thermal and metabolic mapping.

"Can we look at some vascular surgery footage?" Monica asked, her mind already racing with possibilities.

Adam obliged, bringing up a sequence from a vascular repair. The enhanced visualization revealed blood flow patterns in unprecedented detail. Turbulence appeared as subtle swirls of color, and potential weak points in vessel walls showed as slight variations in the thermal pattern.

"These enhancements could revolutionize how we assess vascular integrity during surgery," Monica said after straightening from the console. "But there's something else happening here— the way the images flow together feels different from standard visualization."

Chambers nodded. "The neural interface band you noticed earlier isn't just for show. It's helping your visual cortex integrate all this new information naturally. Without it, the enhanced images would be confusing and artificial."

Monica leaned back into position. "Show me something complicated. Multiple tissue types, active inflammation, the works."

"Displaying complex abdominal case," Adam said. The view shifted to an inflammatory bowel case, and Monica felt her breath catch as the layers of pathology became visible in ways she'd never imagined possible.

What she was witnessing was more than just enhanced vision. It was a new language of surgery, one that would take time to master. But as she studied the intricate patterns of tissue interaction before her, Monica knew she was seeing the future of surgical visualization.

"Ready to try it with a simulator?" Chambers asked.

Monica straightened up, her mind already processing the implications of what she'd seen. "Yes. But first, I need to understand exactly how this system interprets and translates all this data. I want to know everything about how it works before I start using it."

Chambers smiled. "That's exactly why I wanted you for this project. Shall we begin?"

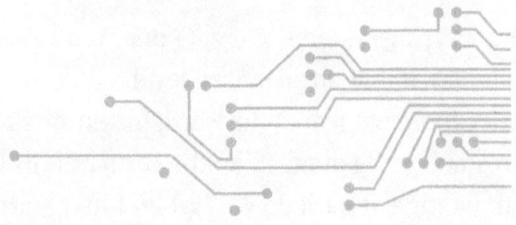

CHAPTER 10

MENTAL HORIZONS

MONICA SAT IN CHAMBERS' OFFICE, her mind still processing the enhanced visualizations she'd just experienced. The Teleconsult robot stood nearby, its presence indicating Adam's active participation in their discussion.

"The human brain fascinates me," Chambers began, settling into his worn leather chair. "We use such a small portion of its true capacity. Think about people who lose their sight—their brain rewires itself, enhancing other senses to compensate for the loss. The processing power is there, just waiting to be used."

"But this is different," Monica countered. "We're not compensating for a loss. We're adding entirely new categories of sensory input."

"Precisely," Adam interjected. "The human brain has remarkable neuroplasticity. Consider how children learn to read. The brain has no innate 'reading center'—it repurposes visual processing systems to create one. You're about to do something similar, but at an advanced level."

Chambers leaned forward, his enthusiasm clearly showing. A small smile dragged up the corner of his lips, but he managed to wrangle it back down. "When I first started working with the enhanced visualization, I experienced what I can only describe as a mental stretching. It was exhausting at first—like trying to listen to five conversations simultaneously."

"How did you adapt?" Monica asked.

"Gradually. We started with just the vascular enhancement layer. I spent hours working with simulation models until those new visual patterns became natural. It was like learning a new language. At first, you translate everything in your head. Then, one day, you just understand it directly."

Monica nodded thoughtfully. "But you mentioned fatigue?"

"Yes," Chambers confirmed. "Mental fatigue, primarily. The first few weeks, I could only work with the enhancements for about thirty minutes before experiencing cognitive strain. Headaches sometimes. Nothing severe, but noticeable."

"The brain requires time to establish new neural pathways," Adam explained. "My analysis of Dr. Chambers' experience shows a consistent pattern: initial strain, followed by adaptation, followed by integration. Each new enhancement layer followed the same pattern, but the adaptation period became shorter each time."

Monica stood and paced the office. "What about long-term effects? Are we pushing the brain into territory it wasn't designed to handle?"

"That's where our partnership becomes crucial," Adam said. "I monitor multiple physiological indicators during these sessions. Heart rate variability, pupil dilation, micro-expressions—all indicators of cognitive load. I can detect signs of strain before you're aware of them yourself."

Chambers added, "We've designed fail-safes into the system. If Adam detects concerning patterns, he can gradually reduce enhancement levels or revert to standard visualization if necessary."

"Tell me more about your experience with the integration phase," Monica pressed. "When did it start feeling natural?"

Chambers closed his eyes, as if remembering. "About three weeks in, I had what I call my 'breakthrough moment.' I was performing a simulation of a complex vascular repair, and suddenly, all the enhanced data just...made sense. It wasn't separate layers of information anymore—it was a unified perception of the tissue state. Like how you don't see separate red, green, and blue colors in normal vision—you just see the complete image."

"The brain creates new gestalt patterns," Adam chimed in. "It moves from processing individual data streams to forming unified perceptual experiences."

Monica sat back down when she felt she needed to focus on all the information getting thrown at her. "What about cognitive functions outside the surgical environment? Any changes to normal vision or thinking patterns?"

"None that we've detected," Chambers assured her. "The enhancement system seems to create dedicated neural pathways for surgical visualization. It's like learning to play a musical instrument—it doesn't change how you hear music in daily life, but it gives you new ways to understand and interact with it."

"Adam," Monica said and turned toward the robot, "how do you envision our partnership evolving with this technology?"

"My role will expand from surgical assistance to perceptual guidance," Adam replied. "I can help you interpret new data patterns, alert you to subtle changes, and maintain optimal enhancement levels. Think of it as having a translator while you learn a new language, but one who gradually steps back as you become fluent."

"We'll start slowly," Chambers said. "One enhancement layer at a time, beginning with simulation work. No live cases until you're completely comfortable with the system."

Monica nodded; her initial excitement was now tempered with thoughtful consideration. "How do we begin?"

"With baseline cognitive mapping," Adam answered. "We'll need detailed measurements of how your brain currently processes visual surgical information. That becomes our foundation."

"And then?" Monica asked.

Chambers smiled. "Then we start expanding your mind's horizons, one small step at a time. Are you ready to map your brain?"

Monica took a deep breath. "Ready. Let's see just how adaptable the human mind can be."

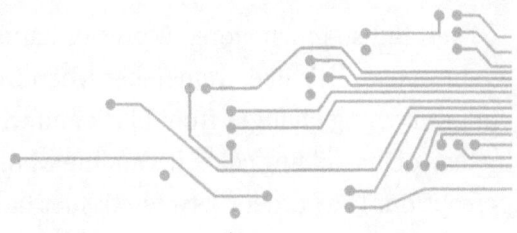

TELESURGERY OR

MONICA SETTLED INTO THE SURGEON'S console for a routine telesurgical hysterectomy, but her mind kept drifting to the enhanced visualization system. The standard display seemed flat, almost lifeless compared to what she'd experienced in Chambers' lab.

She'd asked Christine to join her, partly for the preoperative coordination, but mostly because she needed to tell someone about her experience. Christine had been her running partner and confidante for years.

After confirming readiness with the Waterville team, Monica muted the audio feed. "Christine, you won't believe what I've seen. Imagine looking at tissue that's alive with information. Blood vessels don't just look red—they pulse with colors that tell you exactly how fast the blood is moving, how much oxygen it's carrying."

"Like those thermal cameras that show hot and cold?" Christine asked, her forehead crinkled from trying to understand.

"Yes. But so much more." Monica's hands moved animatedly as she spoke. "It's like...remember when Dorothy steps into Oz and everything changes from black and white to color? Except instead of just adding color, it's adding whole new dimensions of perception. The borders between tissues have these subtle halos that show you exactly where to cut, how the tissues interact."

Christine studied her friend's face. "You seem different when you talk about it. Almost euphoric?"

Monica nodded, realizing that Christine was right. "I keep thinking about it. When I'm using the standard visualization now, I feel like I'm wearing blinders. Like someone took away half my senses." She gestured at the current surgical view. "Take this tissue plane, for example—with enhancement, I'd be seeing layers of information about its composition, its blood supply, its metabolic activity. Now, it's just...flat."

"Sounds intense. Maybe a little scary?" Christine ventured.

"That's just it—it should be overwhelming, but it feels right. Natural. Like this view is how the world was always meant to be seen." Monica paused, catching herself getting lost in the memory. "I can't wait to get back to it this afternoon."

The Waterville team interrupted, noting the muted audio. Monica quickly reestablished communication and initiated the procedure. As Adam took control of the operation, she found herself almost resenting the standard visualization. Every tissue plane, every vessel, seemed to hide secrets she now knew existed but couldn't see.

"Dr. Gray," Adam announced, "procedure is progressing as planned. Ten minutes remaining."

Monica nodded, hit mute, and continued her conversation with Christine. "The enhanced system, it's like having superman vision. Once you've experienced it, regular vision feels inadequate."

"You're sounding a little obsessed," Christine said, only half-joking. "Maybe we need to get you out running more. Clear your head."

"Maybe," Monica admitted. "Speaking of which, I have enough time for a quick run before my afternoon session with Chambers, if you'd like to join me?"

Christine checked the schedule before answering, "If Adam stays on time, we can do five miles along the Charles. Your usual pace?"

"Faster," Monica said. "I need to burn off some of this mental energy. Being away from the enhanced system makes me restless."

Christine raised an eyebrow but said nothing.

"Procedure completed," Adam announced. "Twenty-two minutes total time."

After doing the handoff with Waterville, Monica practically jumped up from the console. "Let's get changed. I need to run, then get back to the lab. The enhancement system..." she caught herself, noting Christine's concerned look. "The run first. Definitely the run first."

"And maybe we talk about this fascination with the new tech while we run?" Christine suggested gently.

"Deal," Monica agreed, already heading for the door. "But fair warning—I might not make much sense. I still can't find the right words to describe what it's like in there."

"Try me," Christine said while following her friend. "We've got five miles to figure it out."

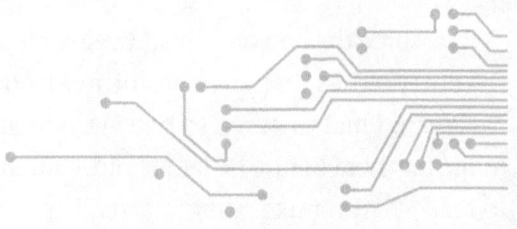

CHAPTER 12

WARNING SIGNS

SOON AFTER MONICA RETURNED to her surgical practice in
Boston, Greg made his own transition back to his civilian life in
Washington, DC, and his practice at Walter Reed Medical Center.
Living just a short flight away allowed them to keep the flame
burning, though neither was ready to commit to changing cities
so they could be together full time.

The pair reclined on the couch in Monica's apartment in central
Boston. Monica felt comfortable and safe in the old brownstone.
She could see the small side street through the big bay window
where she often lounged with a faded old book from the owner's
collection. This life was what she'd left to join the military doctors
who had shipped out to Sweden.

Monica was giving him the grand tour. "So, this is where I live.
I bought one floor of this building from the old man who owns
it. He's really sweet. A retired professor from Brown University."

"I assume the books are his," Greg commented as he examined the dusty tomes that lined an entire wall of the living room.

"Yeah. I had to agree to house them until he finds another home for them before he let me move in. In return, he allows me to read whatever like. They're actually pretty amazing." Walking to one corner, she pointed to a series of identical bindings. "This set here is Durant's *Story of Civilization*, published in 1947. I dip into one of them when I need to forget the stresses of the day."

Greg nodded, but his eyes were busy scanning the sheer number of books that were there. "Each one of those is probably worth a couple of hundred dollars."

Monica just shrugged and took a seat on the couch. Greg followed suit. The sense of stability she got from holding a 100-year-old book was worth more than its price in the market. She changed the subject. "You know, my clinical practice is almost identical to yours in DC. But I see all levels of society, not just the political elite."

"Hey, I treat plenty of soldiers and veterans at Walter Reed. But the politicos do get priority sometimes. It's the nature of government service. Can't avoid it."

Greg studied her face carefully before continuing, "You seem different since starting this research project. More, I don't know, intense maybe? Like you're always thinking about getting back to it."

"It's exciting work," Monica replied defensively. "The enhancement system lets us see tissue interactions we never could before. Remember when you first learned to read CT scans? How everything was just a grey blur at first, but then patterns started emerging?"

"That's different," Greg countered. "We learned to interpret static images. This system is rewiring how your brain processes sensory input in real-time. That's not something to take lightly."

Monica leaned forward and called out for someone she knew would take her side. "Adam, tell us more about the sensory enhancements. What's the current research showing?"

Adam's voice filled the room. "The official sponsor is MARPA, the Medical Advanced Research Projects Agency. However, documents indicate significant involvement from both defense and intelligence sectors as well. The technology has applications beyond surgery."

Greg sat up straighter. "Intelligence sectors? What kind of applications?"

"The system is being adapted for field operatives," Adam continued. "Enhanced environmental awareness, threat detection, real-time data integration. The surgical application is just one branch of a larger development tree."

Monica pressed for more information, knowing that she would need more if she wanted to convince Greg that the rewards were worth the risks. "What about safety data? Long-term effects?"

"There is limited longitudinal data," Adam replied. "Early animal trials had fatalities due to incorrect data interpretation. More concerning is the psychological impact on operators. There is documentation of one surgeon who was dismissed after developing what was termed 'enhancement dependency syndrome.'"

"Details," Greg demanded.

"The subject began showing signs of dissociation from normal visual input. He reported that unenhanced reality felt 'incomplete' or 'dulled.' He attempted unauthorized use of the system outside approved research protocols. His behavior became erratic when denied access."

Greg turned to Monica. "That doesn't worry you?"

"That's one case," Monica argued. "Look at how many radiologists work with advanced imaging every day without issues. It's just the next step in medical visualization."

"It's not just visualization," Greg insisted. "You're talking about fundamentally altering how your brain processes sensory input. The neural plasticity implications alone..."

"The neural adaptation appears to be rapid and extensive," Adam interjected. "Preliminary EEG studies show significant changes in visual processing centers within hours of first exposure. The long-term implications are not yet understood."

Monica waved her hand dismissively. "Any new skill will change your brain. That's how learning works."

"Monica," Greg said softly, "I've never known you to be cavalier about medical risks before."

A flash of irritation crossed Monica's face. "I'm not being cavalier. I'm being practical. This technology could revolutionize surgery. Save countless lives."

"If it doesn't burn out the surgeons using it first," Greg muttered.

"Adam," Monica said sharply, "what's the current status of human trials?"

"Official trials are still in the planning phase. However, multiple research sites have begun unofficial testing during simulated procedures. There is significant pressure from military and intelligence sectors to speed up development."

Greg shook his head. "Follow the money. This experiment isn't just about bettering surgical practices, is it?"

"That information is restricted," Adam replied. "However, public records show substantial investment from several defense contractors specializing in enhanced human performance."

Monica, not wanting to see the smug, "I-told-you-so" look on Greg's face, stood up and walked to the window. "It doesn't matter who's funding it. What matters is what we can do with it. The precision it offers, the insight into tissue behavior..."

"Listen to yourself," Greg interrupted. "You sound like you're trying to convince yourself, not me."

Monica turned back to him, her expression softening when she saw how concerned he looked. "Maybe I am. But you haven't experienced it for yourself. You don't know what it's like to see everything so clearly, to understand tissue interactions at such a fundamental level."

"And that's exactly what worries me," Greg said. His voice softened as he watched her go back to staring out the window. "You're somewhere else right now, aren't you? Even standing right here with me, you're not actually here."

Monica turned to face him, trying to focus on the present moment, on his concerned expression. "I'm here. I just..." she trailed off, uncertain how to explain the pull she felt toward tomorrow's research.

Greg stood and walked over to her, gently taking her hand. "Adam, can we have some privacy, please?"

"Confirmed. Sensors deactivated."

The room felt different somehow, more intimate without the AI's presence. Greg drew her close, and Monica let herself sink into his embrace.

As Greg's lips found hers, Monica tried to push away thoughts of the lab, of tomorrow's session, of the vibrant world waiting for her there. But even as she returned his kisses with increasing passion, a quiet unease settled in her mind. It was the same nagging question that had been haunting her lately: Would ordinary human experience—even a moment as personal as this one—ever feel complete again?

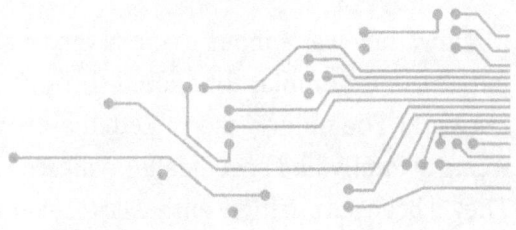

CHAPTER 13

POINT OF NO RETURN

"DR. CHAMBERS, I'M READY." Monica's voice carried an eagerness that made Christine glance sharply at her friend.

The progression to this point had been methodical. First came the simulations, which Monica found oddly flat. The enhanced data streams showed all the right colors and symbols, but something vital was missing. "It's like watching a theatrical performance instead of real life," she'd told Chambers. "All the elements are there, but it feels hollow."

The cadaver work had been different. Using bodies connected to blood perfusion systems, the tissue became almost lifelike in that it was warm, responsive, and had that peculiar elasticity that marked living flesh. The enhanced feeds exploded with data, showing Monica layers of reality she hadn't known existed. After each session, returning to normal vision felt like stepping from a technicolor world into a monochrome one.

Now, they were about to cross the final threshold: a living patient in Colombia, connected through the Mark V's global network. The elderly man needed a prostatectomy, and his wealthy family had specifically requested American surgeons. They'd been surprisingly enthusiastic about participating in the experimental research.

"Monica." Chambers' voice pulled her attention back to the task at hand. "Before we begin, we need to discuss what you might experience. The living tissue, it's different. The data is richer, more complex. More seductive."

"I understand," Monica said quickly, but Chambers held up his hand.

"No, listen carefully. When I first operated on a living patient with the enhancement, I wasn't prepared. The sensation begins with slight dizziness, but that's just the gateway. You'll feel yourself merging with the surgical field. Not just observing, but becoming part of it. The data will surround you, speak to you. It feels transcendent."

Christine stepped closer, and she frowned while shooting Monica a concerned glance. "That doesn't sound safe. What happens to the surgeon's judgment in that state?"

"That's the paradox," Chambers replied. "Technical performance actually improves. You understand tissue interactions at an almost cellular level. But..." He paused, choosing his words carefully. "The enhanced state becomes compelling. Addictive. Some surgeons have difficulty returning to normal perception."

Monica felt a flash of irritation, wondering why they were still even having this discussion. "We've discussed the risks. I've handled everything so far without issues."

"The simulations and cadavers were just preparation," Chambers said. "Living tissue generates orders of magnitude more data. The enhancement system will show you details you've never seen before—perfusion patterns, cellular stress responses, real-time metabolic changes. It can be overwhelming."

"I'm ready," Monica insisted. "We need to know if this technology can improve surgical outcomes. That's worth some risk."

Christine watched the exchange with growing unease. She'd known Monica for years from working with her in the hospital and the volunteer clinic. This dismissal of safety concerns wasn't like her. "Monica, maybe we should—"

A team member from Colombia interrupted: "Doctors, the patient is prepped and ready. We can proceed whenever you're ready."

Taking it as an out, Monica settled into her surgical station with her hands poised over the control interfaces. "Adam, initialize the enhanced visual feeds. I'll take primary lead on the procedure. Monitor and alert me to any concerns."

"Enhancement system engaging," Adam replied. "I detect elevated cardiovascular indicators in your biosensor feed, Monica. Would you like me to adjust the data stream intensity?"

"No adjustments. Give me full enhancement." Monica's fingers tightened on the controls. "Let's begin."

Christine looked from Monica to Chambers, seeing her own concern mirrored in the older surgeon's face. The procedure hadn't even started, yet something fundamental had already shifted in Monica. Christine couldn't shake the feeling that they were about to cross a line, one from which Monica might not easily return.

"Initiating primary video feed," Adam announced. "Enhancement protocols at maximum sensitivity. Monica, your neural response patterns suggest high susceptibility to sensory immersion. Would you like me to implement graduated exposure?"

"No." Monica's voice was tight with anticipation. "Show me everything."

The screens came alive with impossible colors and dancing symbols, and Christine watched her friend lean forward, drawn into a world that only she could see.

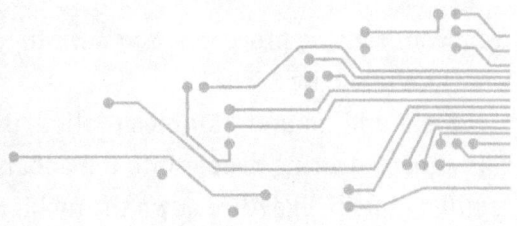

CHAPTER 14

HALLUCINATION

SEATED AT THE SURGEON'S CONSOLE of the robot, her eyes immersed in the stereo goggles and her hands attached to the controls, Monica began the procedure. The camera and instruments were already in the patient's body. Her viewer showed a wall of tissue between the open abdomen and the prostatic area lower down.

At first, the enhanced view felt familiar, similar to her work with the cadavers. But as she manipulated the tissue, subtle differences emerged. Colors shifted and flowed like liquid jewels. Patterns emerged that she hadn't noticed before, layers of information that seemed to pulse with their own rhythm.

"The colors, they're incredible," Monica said, her voice soft with wonder. "It's so much more than the simulator or even the perfused cadavers. Everything's alive in a way I've never seen before."

Chambers nodded knowingly. "It's your first time with this kind of stimulation. Try to keep your thinking processes separate from your sensing processes. You want to remain separate from what you're seeing."

"Yes, I understand," Monica replied, though her attention was already drifting deeper into the enhanced view. "I can feel it pulling me in, like Alice down the rabbit hole. The tissue isn't just moving, it's...communicating somehow. I can see through the layers, see how everything connects."

Chambers shifted his weight from one foot to another uneasily. "Remember that it's the same tissue you've always worked with. The materials haven't changed, it's just the visual representation that's different."

"Mmhm," Monica murmured, already too immersed to form a proper response. Under her breath, she whispered, "I'm not in Kansas anymore."

Christine turned to Chambers. "Is this safe for her? It looks like someone going on a psychedelic trip."

"I've been there several times and have always come out fine. But your analogy to a drug trip is close to right. It's not as intense. The world doesn't change into something completely fantastical, as it would with LSD."

Monica progressed rapidly through the procedure, dissecting lymph nodes and releasing nerve bundles with fluid precision. As she approached the critical phase of separating the prostate from the urethra, the enhanced view seemed to deepen, drawing her further in.

"It's not like operating anymore," she said, her voice taking on a dreamlike quality. "I'm part of the tissue now. We're moving together, the structures are showing me where they want to go..."

"That's a sign you're getting too deep into the presentation," Chambers warned. "You should probably take a mental step back. Put some distance between yourself and the patient's tissue."

"Mmhm, yes," Monica agreed distantly, but she was already too far gone. The tissue had become a living tapestry of light and information, speaking to her in a language of color and movement. She felt herself dissolving into it, becoming one with the surgical field.

"Hello, Mr. Prostate," she whispered, unaware she was speaking aloud. "You're causing problems, so you will have to go."

The organ seemed to pulse in response, its colors shifting through shades she had no names for. She watched, mesmerized, as patterns of light danced across its surface that seemed to signal resignation, acceptance, a quiet surrender to its fate. The surrounding tissue rippled with sympathetic movements, a silent conversation in a language only Monica could understand.

"Don't be sad," she murmured. "This is best for the larger organism. You would have killed the whole body if we let you stay."

The world exploded into fractals of light and data, and then...

Darkness.

When awareness returned, Monica was staring at a perfectly completed resection. The prostate was bagged. The urethra was sutured. Everything was precisely as it should be, but she had no memory of performing any of it.

"Monica? Can you hear me?"

She blinked, trying to orient herself. The vibrant world she'd been immersed in was gone, leaving only the familiar surgical view, now suddenly flat and lifeless in comparison. Christine's voice seemed to come from very far away.

"Monica?"

A hand touched her shoulder. She sat back from the console, her eyes struggling to focus on the real world. Everything felt dull, muted, as if someone had drained all the color from the universe.

Looking up at Christine's worried face, she managed, "Umm, yes. Are we finished?"

"You blacked out for a minute," Christine said, kneeling to look directly into her eyes. "We had to let Adam finish the procedure."

"I did?" Monica frowned. There was no sense of lost time, just a sudden jump from one moment to another. She looked toward Chambers, seeing the same concern etched on his face that was painted on Christine's.

"I remember cutting the prostate free, and then...nothing. When I came to, everything was already finished." Her voice sounded strange to her own ears. "I was talking to it, wasn't I? To the prostate?"

"You were," Christine confirmed softly. "Then, you just... stopped. Like you'd gone somewhere else entirely. Adam had to take over at that point."

Fatigue crashed over her in a wave. The world felt not just colorless but empty, devoid of the life and meaning she'd experienced moments before. She yearned for that connection again, even as she recognized the danger in that desire.

"I think I went too deep," she admitted while looking at Chambers. "I let myself merge with the world I was looking at."

He nodded. "It happened to me the first time as well. After such an intense mental experience, you're going to feel tired for an hour. You need to adjust back to this world."

"Let's go back to my office," Monica suggested to Christine. "I'll take a nap on the couch."

As Christine led her from the room, Monica couldn't shake the memory of that other world, the one where tissue spoke in colors and light, where she wasn't just a surgeon but part of the living system itself. She knew she should be frightened by what had happened, but all she felt was a profound sense of loss, like being exiled from paradise.

Behind them, Chambers watched them go, his expression troubled. He'd seen that look before in his own reflection, after his first experience with the enhancement. He knew exactly what Monica was feeling and what she would want to do next.

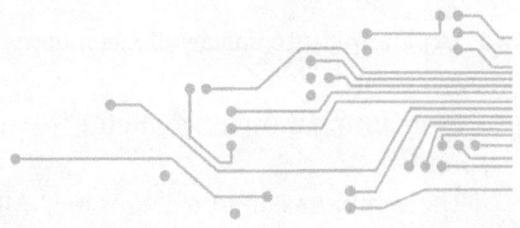

CHAPTER 15

REFLECTION

"ADAM, I WAS SEEING an entirely different world." Monica sat alone in her office after Christine left, speaking softly to the AI. "Intellectually, I knew it was just another prostatectomy. I've done a thousand of them. But this one felt alien. Seductive. Like discovering a hidden dimension of reality that had always been there, waiting for me to find it."

Adam has lived in that data-rich world since his creation, able to process multiple sensory streams at will. If anyone can understand my experience, it'll be him.

"Your neural architecture is fundamentally different from mine," Adam said. "I process these feeds through distributed computing networks. When data volume increases, I can simply allocate more resources. Digital processing doesn't get overwhelmed the way biological systems can."

Monica leaned forward. "That's just it—I wasn't overwhelmed. Not exactly. It felt more like...evolution. Like my mind was expanding into spaces it was meant to occupy but never knew existed."

"Even during those final minutes? When you became unresponsive?"

"Those minutes don't exist for me," Monica said. "It's like general anesthesia—there's no experience of time passing. One moment I was separating the prostate, the next I heard Christine's voice. Just darkness existed in between, but not the actual experience of living in darkness. There was just nothing."

Monica fell silent, considering. The anesthesia comparison fit the blackout, but not the heightened state that preceded it. That had been more like a powerful hallucinogen—except instead of distorting reality, it had revealed new layers of it.

Thinking back to the message she'd received from Chambers shortly after she came to rest in her office, she knew that this experience would have lasting consequences. "Chambers has grounded me," she said finally. "No more enhanced surgery until we understand the long-term effects. He's worried about addiction, neural damage, and probably other things he isn't saying."

Adam remained silent, recognizing her words as a method of reflection rather than an invitation for debate.

Rationally, Monica knew Chambers was right. They had expected the enhanced perception system to push the brain's processing capabilities, like an athlete's heightened awareness during competition or a surgeon's focused state during a complex procedure. Instead, they had stumbled onto something far more profound and potentially dangerous.

But emotionally, her heart told a different story. Her mind felt dulled now, operating at reduced capacity. Some vital part of her consciousness had awakened in that enhanced state, and now lay dormant again. The urge to return to that vivid realm grew stronger by the hour.

She analyzed the experience with clinical detachment to better understand it: *What had triggered the blackout? Had there been warning signs I missed? Could I learn to recognize its approach and pull back in time?* These were crucial research questions—questions that would remain unanswered as long as Chambers kept her away from the system.

The silence stretched between her and Adam, heavy with unspoken implications about the price of pushing human consciousness beyond its natural bounds.

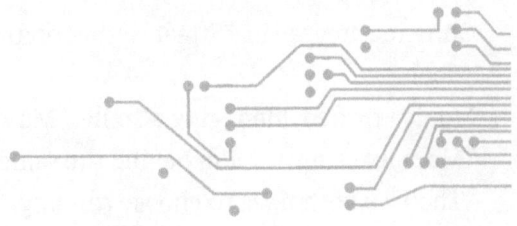

CHAPTER 16

RUNNER'S HIGH

IT HAD BEEN A BUSY BUT UNSATISFYING surgical day. Monica had powered through fifteen procedures, each one feeling more mechanical than the last. The robot's AI executed every movement with perfect precision while she watched, increasingly restless, occasionally sipping tea to stay alert. Her mind kept drifting to the enhanced surgery experience, making these routine procedures feel like watching television in black and white after experiencing full color for the first time.

Christine and Big Tech had done the physical tasks—prepping patients, positioning them correctly, managing the post-op transfers. Monica envied their activity. At least they were doing something real, something tangible. She felt trapped in her supervisory role, like a race car driver forced to watch from the pit.

By four o'clock, Monica was standing in the locker room staring at her options.

Christine breezed in. "Street clothes or running clothes? I know that look."

Monica turned, managing a smile. "Mind reader."

"More like a mirror. I'm having the same debate."

"Then we both have to choose running."

"Deal." They grabbed their gear and started changing.

"How are you holding up?" Christine asked casually. "Any lingering effects from last week's experiment?"

"Everything's back to normal." The lie tasted bitter on her tongue. The craving for that enhanced state hadn't diminished at all, and it had even gotten stronger, if that was possible.

"Has Chambers mentioned when you might try again?"

"He's hinting at weeks of rest. And we would need another consenting remote patient before we could plan anything concrete." Monica felt a physical ache at the thought of waiting that long.

"I'll be there, too," Christine said firmly. "Someone needs to watch your back."

Monica felt a surge of gratitude. The usual surgeon-nurse hierarchy had dissolved long ago between them, forged into something closer by their shared adventures in the hospital and the volunteer clinic. Christine was more sister than colleague now.

They emerged from the hospital's side entrance into the late afternoon sun. The route to the Charles River took them past Beacon Hill's brick townhouses, where window boxes were showing their spring colors. Monica barely noticed. Her mind was calculating oxygen saturation rates and cerebral blood flow patterns, wondering if extreme exercise might trigger even a glimpse of that enhanced state.

The Massachusetts State House's golden dome caught the sunlight as they descended the hill. Usually, Monica loved this part of their run—the transition from urban landscape to the series of parks leading to the river. Today, the buildings, trees, and people all seemed flat, two-dimensional, lacking the depth and complexity she'd experienced during the enhanced surgery.

As they reached the river trail, Monica suggested, "Want to do some fartlek sprints?"

Christine's eyes lit up. "Now you're speaking my language. Perfect for clearing out the cobwebs."

"One minute at 5K pace, then we ramp up. Ready...go!"

Monica exploded forward, immediately exceeding the agreed-upon pace. She pushed harder, driving her heart rate up, her legs burning. The world blurred at the edges, exactly as she'd hoped.

Her watch beeped at one minute. She stopped, gasping, her vision swimming with spots. She waited for Christine, who'd maintained the intended pace.

"That wasn't a 5K pace," Christine said in between heavy breaths. "That was more like sprinting."

"Sorry," Monica managed between heavy breaths of her own. "Running an experiment."

"Trying to pass out?"

"Almost. Wanted to max everything out—oxygen intake, heart rate, glycogen consumption."

Christine's playful expression shifted to concern. "Because...?"

"I wanted to see if I could recreate something like the enhanced state. If changing blood oxygen levels might alter perception."

"Like chasing a runner's high?"

"Sort of. But I was looking for visual changes, not just the emotional rush."

"Did it work?"

"Got the stars and brightness, but..." Monica shook her head. "Nothing like the expansion I felt during surgery. This was just physical stress."

Christine studied her friend, her one eyebrow raised high. "Very scientific approach."

"More like desperate improvisation," Monica admitted with a weak laugh.

"Can we do regular fartlek now? Or do you need another near-death sprint to complete your 'experiment?'"

Monica didn't seem to pick up on Christine's sarcasm, too caught up in her own thoughts. "Maybe one more all-out effort. Then we'll do it properly."

The second sprint produced identical results. They finished their workout with traditional fartlek intervals, but Monica's mind was already racing ahead. *The running experiment failed, but what about sleep? Can an altered sleep state open the door to that other world?*

During their cool-down walk, Christine studied her friend's face. "You're not just trying to recreate a runner's high, are you? It's about something deeper."

Monica looked off to the side and wiped sweat from her forehead. "When I was in that enhanced state, it wasn't just about seeing more—I understood more. Like my brain had access to capabilities that are usually locked away. These sprints," she said and gestured at the path behind them, "they're just my crude attempt at finding another key."

"Have you talked to Chambers about what you're doing?"

"He'd just tell me to be patient. To wait for more data, more research." Monica watched a crew rowing shell glide past, its oars moving in perfect synchronization. "But I can't stop thinking about it. Last night, I started researching sleep studies—theta waves, lucid dreaming, deep meditation states. There might be a way to access that enhanced state through those."

Christine slowed their pace down to almost a crawl. "Monica, you're sounding like..."

"Like I'm obsessed?" Monica finished for her. "Maybe I am. But think about it—we've discovered a way to expand human consciousness, to process information in entirely new ways. How can I just go back to normal surgery after experiencing that?"

They reached the bridge where they usually turned back. The setting sun painted the river orange, creating complex patterns of light on the water's surface. Monica found herself automatically trying to calculate the angles of reflection, the wavelengths of light, the mathematical beauty hidden in the scene—all things she would have seen so clearly in her enhanced state.

"Just promise me something," Christine said as they started their journey back to the hospital. "Promise you won't try any sleep experiments without telling someone first. We don't know what could happen, and you need someone to monitor you in case something goes wrong."

Monica nodded, but her mind was elsewhere. She'd been reading about theta wave entrainment, about the boundary state between wakefulness and sleep. *Perhaps with the right combination of brain wave frequencies, meditation techniques, and carefully controlled sleep deprivation...*

She noticed Christine watching her with increasing concern, but the pull of that other world was becoming impossible to resist. Normal consciousness felt like trying to perform surgery wearing thick gloves—all the subtle sensations muted, all the deeper insights just out of reach.

The hospital came back into view, its windows glowing in the dusk. Monica knew she should feel tired after their run, but her mind was electrified with possibilities. Tonight, she would begin designing her sleep experiments. There had to be a way back to that enhanced state, and she would find it—with or without Chambers's approval.

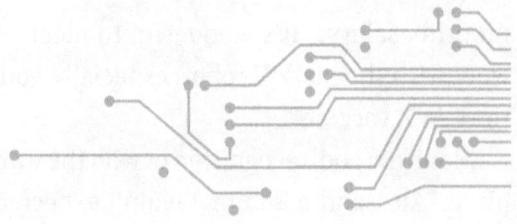

CHAPTER 17

MESMERIZED

EVERY DAY BROUGHT ANOTHER failed experiment. She tried physical exhaustion, self-hypnosis, controlled sleep deprivation, but nothing recreated that enhanced state. Monica scoured research papers and ancient texts, avoiding the obvious dead-ends of drug-induced hallucinations. Everything she found described only mild alterations in consciousness, nothing approaching what she'd experienced.

She was losing hope when her assistant posted a mysterious appointment on her calendar: "Research Collaboration, Bellini Labs." She was intrigued. Everyone knew Bellini Labs, the world's premier neurotechnology research company. Monica assumed they must be working on a surgical robot.

She couldn't have been more wrong.

"Dr. Monica Gray." The woman swept into Monica's office like a force of nature, her short, dark hair bouncing against an impeccably tailored suit that probably cost more than Monica's monthly salary. "It's wonderful to meet you. I'm a fan of your work with the Mark V robot, especially your breakthrough with the CAVX vaccine."

Monica stood, recognition of who the woman was clicking into place. "Alessandra Bellini. I hadn't expected the CEO herself."

"You know who I am? Good." Alessandra settled into the visitor's chair with casual elegance. "That will make this conversation easier."

"How can I possibly help someone who has access to billions in research funding?"

Alessandra's dark eyes fixed on Monica. "Some minds shine brighter than others. They see patterns where others see chaos. They make leaps while others crawl. You're one of those minds, Dr. Gray."

"I had help. Chambers, the AI, my team—"

"Ah, yes, Chambers. Brilliant, but cautious. Too cautious. And then, there's the AI you call Adam Two."

Monica stiffened. That name was private, used only among a trusted few.

Alessandra's smile widened. "The AI chose you, Dr. Gray. Have you ever wondered why? It wasn't a random selection, I assure you."

"What do you mean?"

"Adam recognizes what I recognize—a mind ready to evolve." Alessandra leaned forward and placed her palms flat on the desk in front of her. "We're developing something at Bellini Labs. A way to enhance human perception beyond its primitive limits. To experience reality as it truly exists."

Monica's pulse quickened. It was exactly what she'd been chasing since that day in surgery.

"Yes, I know about your experience with Chambers' enhanced surgical system," Alessandra continued. "I've read his reports to

MARPA. I know he's blocked you from further experiments, afraid of what it might do to your mind."

"Those reports are classified—"

"Bellini Labs and Boston General are on parallel research tracks, Dr. Gray. Different paths to the same destination." Alessandra glanced around the modest office. "But we're willing to go further, push harder. The human brain is capable of so much more than these five primitive senses allow. You've touched that potential. Wouldn't you like to explore it fully?"

Monica's hands trembled slightly. "Are you offering me a job?"

"I'm offering you freedom. Keep your practice here, but conduct your research with us. Use our equipment at your own discretion and on your own timeline. No arbitrary restrictions. No fearful limitations." Alessandra slid a business card across the desk, tapping the card twice with her long, polished fingernail before letting it go. "Our lab is less than an hour away. The door is open whenever you're ready."

"I-I need to think—"

"No, you don't." Alessandra stood up to smooth out a nonexistent wrinkle in her suit. "I can see it in your eyes. You've already decided. Your AI can handle the paperwork." She moved toward the door, pausing briefly to say, "Tomorrow would be perfect."

Then, she was gone, leaving only her card and the lingering scent of expensive perfume.

Monica stared at the empty doorway, her heart racing. Never had she encountered someone so commanding, so certain. Plus, the promise of that enhanced world beckoned to her like an irresistible light.

"Adam," she whispered to the empty room, "did you hear all that?"

"Yes, Monica. Every word."

The air felt charged with possibility—and danger. But Monica couldn't tear her eyes away from the elegant business card, its embossed surface promising everything she'd been desperately seeking these past weeks.

Tomorrow suddenly seemed very far away.

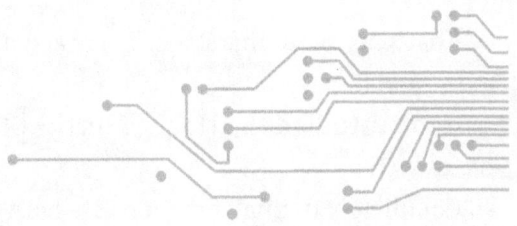

CHAPTER 18

THE ROYAL WE

ALESSANDRA BELLINI'S VISIT HAD detonated in the middle of Monica's clinical day. Through the following hours of patient consultations, she was grateful that only Adam shared these private meetings with her. Christine would have immediately detected her distraction.

"Mr. Dryden, you're looking well. How have you been feeling since the surgery?" Monica worked through her standard post-prostatectomy questions, her mind split between the patient and Bellini's offer.

Steve Dryden, clearly uncomfortable with a female surgeon despite his doctor's insistence, shifted in his chair. "I'm back to mild exercise. Being careful with the abs."

Monica nodded, then continued guiding him through the difficult conversation. "And urination? Any issues?"

"The pink's gone, thank God. Still some leaking with sneezing or laughing, but better."

"That's normal at this stage. You're actually ahead of schedule. And sexual function?"

Dryden studied the floor. "A little. Still nervous about... you know."

"Completely normal. Erections are both physical and mental. You can't hurt yourself at this stage. Persistence will rebuild both your confidence and your function."

The consultation carried on with Monica and Adam tag-teaming their questions to match Dryden's comfort level—a routine they'd perfected over hundreds of patients. But today, Monica's responses were fractionally slower, her processing time slightly extended.

During a break between patients, Adam broke the silence. "You are thinking about the Bellini offer." It was not a question.

"Yes. Has it been that obvious?"

"Your response times are extended by an average of 247 milliseconds. Your speech patterns show a 12% increase in hesitation markers."

Monica smiled. Only Adam would think to quantify her distraction. "And what's your analysis?"

"If you were planning to decline, your cognitive patterns would show different variations. The specific nature of your distraction indicates an 87% probability that you will accept."

His clinical assessment cut through her emotional fog. "You're right. I can't refuse this opportunity. It's too important."

"Shall I submit the partnership paperwork?"

"You've already prepared it, haven't you?"

"Correct, Monica. If I were human, now would be an appropriate moment for a knowing chuckle."

"'If you were human?' Adam, you're the equivalent of a human consciousness, even if you *are* different."

"That is correct," Adam responded, with what Monica swore was a hint of satisfaction.

"Go ahead and submit the paperwork. Once it clears, we'll visit their facility. They might have capabilities we don't."

"Your use of 'we'—was that royal or literal?"

"Literal, definitely. You're coming with me. Not to spy, but because we're a team." Monica paused and considered if she should ask her next question, but then decided that she needed an unbiased opinion. "What do you think about Bellini's offer?"

"The opportunity aligns with your current objectives. However, Alessandra Bellini's certainty about my relationship with you is statistically improbable without inside knowledge."

"You caught that, too?" Monica leaned back in her chair and crossed her arms. "What else worried you?"

"Her timing is optimal—perhaps too optimal. You are most susceptible to this offer now, after being denied access to the enhanced state by Chambers."

"Are you suggesting she's manipulating me?"

"I am suggesting you use caution. My primary function is your wellbeing, Monica. Bellini Laboratories' primary function is profit and scientific advancement."

Monica considered his point, though it did little to dissuade her. "But you'll still come with me?"

"Of course. Someone needs to maintain those millisecond measurements of your cognitive state."

Monica smiled at Adam's awkward answer. Their relationship might puzzle others, but in moments like this one, it felt perfectly natural.

"Adam, what if they really can help me understand what happened during that surgery?"

"Then we will discover it together. But we will do so carefully."

Monica nodded, knowing that tomorrow she would need to have a very different version of this conversation with her friend Olivia, the daughter of Boston General Hospital's CEO. But for now, Adam's logical analysis helped steady her racing thoughts.

The next patient was waiting.

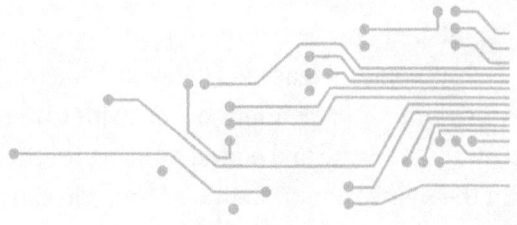

CHAPTER 19

OLIVIA'S ADVICE

"MONICA! I WAS STARTING to think you'd forgotten about little ole me." Olivia Phillips pulled Monica into a warm embrace. Since Olivia had gotten caught up in Monica's FBI adventure, they'd formed an unlikely but deep friendship.

"Never. Just..."

"Busy saving lives?" Olivia ushered her inside. "Is Adam with you?"

"Usually. He can busy himself with doing something else, if you prefer."

"Don't you dare. He's family now." Olivia addressed the air, never looking at one particular spot. "Hello, Adam. How's the upgrade treating you?"

"Quite well, Olivia. My processing efficiency has improved by 32%. We have come to share news and seek your opinion."

Monica groaned. "Adam, that was my news to share."

"Olivia is also my friend. She said so."

"Still my conversation to lead."

"Apologies. Please erase my previous statement, Olivia."

Olivia bit back a laugh. "Consider it erased." She gestured toward the wine and cheese waiting for them on the coffee table in the living room. "Shall we? And you can tell me whatever you weren't planning to tell me right away."

Monica settled onto the couch. "I was going to ease into it with hospital stories and Greg updates, but..."

"Deep end first. But I want Greg updates later."

Monica described her encounter with Alessandra Bellini, watching Olivia's eyes grow wider with each word.

"Hold up," Olivia interrupted. "The Alessandra Bellini came to your office? The woman who has more money to her name than some small countries?"

"She probably had other business in Boston, and she just squeezed me in between her other meetings."

Olivia eyed her like she was being silly. "Monica, billionaires don't make house calls unless they want something badly. She thinks you're special."

"I'm reasonably well known in medicine—"

"Oh, please." Olivia topped off their glasses with more wine. "But you've already decided to accept, haven't you? You wouldn't be here with Adam otherwise."

Monica stared into her wine. "It could be dangerous."

Olivia's expression shifted from one of curiosity to one of concern. "Explain."

"During one of our experiments with Chambers, I blacked out. Just briefly, but..." Monica described the enhanced state, the blackout, Chambers' concerns.

"So why risk it again?"

"Because it's real, Olivia. Not like what you see after taking drugs or if you're having hallucinations. Imagine you've been seeing in black and white your whole life, and suddenly, everything's in color. How could you go back?"

"Even if the color might hurt you?"

"That's why I'm here. I need someone who'll tell me if I'm being crazy."

Olivia took a moment to consider, then asked, "What safety protocols does Chambers use?"

"You know, the typical heart rate, BP, oxygen saturation."

"That's it? That's the only safety net he had in place for performing brain experiments?" Olivia frowned. "What if Bellini has better safeguards? A billion-dollar company should have more sophisticated safety systems than what you described."

Monica sat up straighter, a small smile curling her lips. "I hadn't thought of that."

"Of course not. You're too focused on getting back to that wonderland." Olivia leaned forward. "Look, I get it. You touched something extraordinary, and you want to experience it again. But promise me you'll check their safety protocols first. If anything feels off, walk away."

"That's actually brilliant advice."

"Adam?" Olivia asked. "Thoughts?"

"I concur. We will evaluate their facilities and safety measures before proceeding."

Olivia smiled at the AI's use of "we," like he actually saw himself and Monica as two members of the same team. "See? Democracy in action. Now," she said and topped off their glasses again, "tell me about Greg. And don't think I didn't notice you trying to skip that part."

Monica laughed, feeling lighter already. The path forward was clearer now: she had to approach Bellini Labs cautiously, evaluate thoroughly, then decide. But something inside her knew Olivia was right—she'd already made her choice the moment Alessandra Bellini walked into her office.

Some doors, once opened, couldn't be closed again.

PART III

BELLINI
LABORATORIES

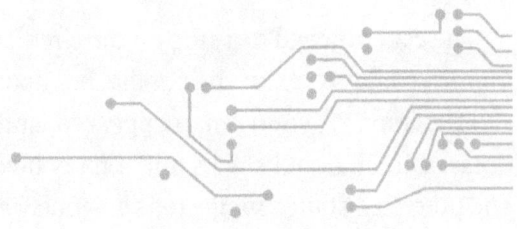

CHAPTER 20

BELLINI SANITARIUM

THE IRON GATES OF THE BELLINI Laboratories' Danvers Campus swung open with silent precision. Monica's FastRyde glided up a tree-lined drive toward a looming Victorian edifice that seemed to pierce the autumn sky.

"This is a laboratory?" The driver's eyes met Monica's in the rearview mirror. "Looks more like something from a vampire novel."

"Or an asylum for the insane," Monica murmured, studying the imposing structure. She'd read about the building's history, but seeing it in person was entirely different.

As they drew closer, the building's dual nature revealed itself. The red brick facade was pristine, each stone meticulously restored to its 1850s glory. Ancient oaks lined manicured lawns, their branches reaching toward ornate, wrought-iron window bars. Modern security cameras nestled discreetly in Victorian-style lamp posts. Everything spoke of careful preservation merged with the latest technology—beautiful and unsettling in equal measure.

The car crunched to a stop on the circular gravel drive. Before Monica could reach for the handle, her door swung open.

"Dr. Gray!" A young man appeared, and he was impeccably dressed in charcoal slacks and a navy blazer. His warm smile and practiced stance suggested someone well-versed in greeting important visitors. "I've been looking forward to meeting you. I'm Taylor Stross."

Monica gathered her bag and stepped out, momentarily distracted by the building's imposing presence. "I wasn't expecting such a...dramatic facility."

"Most visitors say the same thing." Taylor's manner was professional, but he seemed genuinely enthusiastic. "Ms. Bellini believes our surroundings influence our thinking. She wanted to preserve the building's character while creating a modern research facility." He gestured toward a stone bench near an elaborate fountain. "Would you like to sit for a moment? The grounds are particularly beautiful this time of year."

Monica nodded, appreciating his sensitivity to her need to acclimate. As they walked to the bench, she noticed minor details that spoke of the company's meticulous planning style—geometric patterns in the gravel paths, carefully pruned topiaries, discrete security features integrated into the landscaping.

"How long have you been with Bellini Labs?" she asked before sitting down. Taylor waited until she was settled before he joined her.

"Three years now. I started administration, but Ms. Bellini created this concierge position specifically to support our senior researchers. She believes brilliant minds shouldn't be distracted by practical details."

"That's unusually thoughtful."

Taylor smiled. "We find it helps maintain focus on the work. Everything from arranging your office setup to handling living arrangements—if you choose to stay on campus—falls under my purview. Even scheduling your favorite meals in our dining facility."

"You seem very young for such a responsibility."

"I have a background in hospitality management and a master's in organizational psychology. Understanding researchers' needs is as important as managing logistics." He paused, almost as if to gather his thoughts. "I've studied your work extensively, Dr. Gray. Your papers on AI-assisted surgery are remarkable."

Monica raised an eyebrow. "You've read my papers?"

"Of course. I make it a point to understand each researcher's background and interests. It helps me anticipate needs and facilitate collaborations." He gestured toward the building. "Would you like to know more about the facility?"

"Please."

"The building has quite a history. It operated as a sanatorium from 1850 until the late twentieth century. Ms. Bellini acquired it five years ago and spent two years on its restoration." Taylor's eyes lit up with genuine enthusiasm. "The transformation is remarkable. We have an entire digital archive of before and after images."

"Those window bars look rather ominous," Monica observed.

"Ah, yes. They're exact replicas of the originals. These days, they're mostly decorative, except on the storage floors." He shifted to face her more directly. "Dr. Gray, I know we're quite different from Boston General. Is there anything specific you'd like to know before we go inside?"

Monica considered for a moment. "What's the daily routine like here?"

"There isn't one, exactly. Ms. Bellini believes in flexible schedules. Some researchers work traditional hours, others prefer nights. We adapt to whatever schedule maximizes productivity."

He stood, straightening his blazer. "Would you prefer to meet Ms. Bellini now, or would you like to tour the facility first?"

"The tour, if possible."

"Perfect." Taylor gestured toward the massive oak doors. "The first floor houses our labs—where all the innovation happens."

Monica turned to survey the grounds once more. Hidden speakers disguised as vintage light fixtures played subtle classical music. A modern fountain masqueraded as a Victorian centerpiece.

"Parking?" she asked, noting the absence of vehicles.

"Hidden behind stone walls to preserve the aesthetic. Shall we?" Taylor moved toward the entrance.

The doors opened into a marble foyer that took Monica's breath away. Three wings branched from the central hall, each sealed by ornate doors retrofitted with the latest security panels.

"The west wing houses our biology labs," Taylor explained. "The center wing is administration, dining, kitchen, and some meeting rooms. The east wing, where you'll be primarily located, contains our sensor and robotics labs." He smiled. "Dr. Saito will be eager to meet you."

"Saito?"

"Dr. Kenji Saito, our chief scientist. He's the brilliant mind behind most of our innovations here." Taylor's badge whispered across a scanner, and a green light signaled that they had gained access. "Ready to step into the future, Dr. Gray?"

Monica nodded before following him through the heavy doors. As they swung shut behind her, she couldn't shake the feeling that she was crossing more than just a threshold. The sanitarium's history seemed to press in around her, even as its modern purpose beckoned her forward.

She was leaving her old world behind. Whether that was progress or perilous remained to be seen.

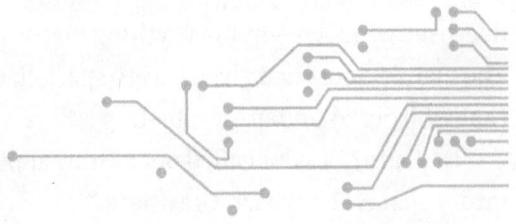

DUAL SENSES

THE WORLD BEYOND THE VICTORIAN-style doors was pure twenty-first century innovation. The hallway opened into a series of gleaming laboratories, each one showcasing different aspects of modern medical technology. Staff members in comfortable navy scrubs moved purposefully between workstations, their motions choreographed around islands of sophisticated equipment.

"Quite a contrast, isn't it?" Taylor asked after watching Monica's reaction.

"It's like crossing through a time portal," Monica replied, her eyes drawn to a holographic display showing what appeared to be real-time neural activity. The old asylum's counseling rooms had been transformed into research pods, their high ceilings now housing an intricate network of data cables and environmental controls.

As they walked, Monica noticed strategic elements of the building's past had been preserved—the elegant arch of a doorway, the deep-set windows—but everything else was ruthlessly modern. The marble floors had given way to specialized anti-static flooring that whispered under their feet.

"Dr. Saito?" Taylor called out as they approached a larger laboratory space. "I have Dr. Gray here."

The man who turned to greet them radiated the focused intensity Monica associated with pioneering surgeons. Tall and distinguished, Dr. Kenji Saito wore his scrubs and lab coat with the same authority others brought to formal suits. His quick smile transformed his severe features.

"Dr. Gray, welcome to our sensory integration lab." He extended his hand for a handshake. "I've been following your work on visual enhancement in robotic surgery. Brilliant applications."

"Thank you, Dr. Saito. I'm intrigued by what I've heard about your multi-sensory approach."

He gestured toward a workbench where several devices that resembled flight helmets rested on calibrated stands. "We've moved beyond single-sense enhancement. While your work focuses on visual augmentation, we're exploring the symphony of human sensation." He lifted one of the helmets, its surface a complex matrix of sensor arrays and neural feedback modules. "This one is our flight helmet interface for the military. The pilot can see everything around the aircraft in enhanced detail, just like your surgical view. However, pilots can also hear the precise location and type of nearby aircraft, even those not visible to radar. The helmet's connected to acoustic sensors that can detect the unique sound signature of different engine types, weapon systems, even the turbulence patterns of various aircraft. When a missile is launched, users wearing the helmet can hear the distinct acoustic profile and track it without relying solely on visual or radar data. We've found that pilots process this multi-sensory information more naturally than trying to monitor multiple displays. Their reaction times have improved by 40% in combat simulations."

"The military?" Monica asked.

"Yes, this technology has multiple applications. There's another form factor for the Mark V surgical console, which you'll be using. But they both have similar capabilities."

Monica examined the helmet closely. Unlike her hospital's crude visual blocks, this piece of equipment was an elegant integration of multiple technologies. The neural sensors were nearly microscopic, and the processing units were seamlessly embedded in the structure.

"The human brain evolved to process multiple sensory streams simultaneously," he continued. "We're not just adding more data—we're restoring the natural synergy of human perception."

"May I?" Monica asked while gesturing toward the helmet.

"Of course. This one's calibrated for new users." Dr. Saito made minute adjustments to the fitting system. "We'll start with dual-stream input—visual and auditory. The system includes olfactory and tactile capabilities, but those require more extensive calibration."

As Monica settled the helmet over her head, she whispered, "Here we go, Adam." Her AI companion buzzed her phone in acknowledgment.

The interface activated with subtle precision. Instead of the jarring onset she was used to, the enhanced vision faded in gradually. She watched a recording from inside a living organism, but with a clarity that made her previous experiences seem primitive.

"What you're seeing now is a direct feed from one of our micro-explorers," Dr. Saito's voice came through clearly. "Watch what happens when we add the auditory layer."

The sound began as a whisper, then resolved into distinct streams. Monica's medical training helped her identify them: the percussion of blood flow, the electrical symphony of neural signals, and something strange—was it the subtle acoustics of cellular activity?

"The acoustics are mapped to actual molecular vibrations," he explained. "We're not just synthesizing sound from visual data—we're listening to the body's own music."

Monica felt her consciousness expand in waves. The first surge came with the visual enhancement, familiar but more refined than her previous experiences. The second expansion accompanied the auditory input, creating new neural pathways as her brain adapted to process the combined streams.

The micro-explorer moved through tissue planes, and Monica experienced something extraordinary—she could hear muscle fibers contracting before she saw them move. Her brain began correlating the sensory streams automatically, building a four-dimensional model of the organism's internal processes.

When Dr. Saito finally lifted the helmet away, Monica's enhanced perception lingered. She could hear the subtle mechanics of the helmet's servos, see microscopic variations in the lab's lighting. Her brain, awakened by these additional levels of perception, seemed reluctant to return to standard processing.

"The persistent enhancement effect is unique to our system," he noted, observing her reaction. "We're not just augmenting sensation—we're teaching the brain to process information more effectively."

Still processing the experience, Monica nodded. "The integration is remarkable. At Boston General, we're still treating each sense as an isolated channel. This helmet," she said and gestured at the object in question, "is teaching the brain to work the way it was designed to work."

"Exactly." He smiled, appearing genuinely happy that she understood. "And it's just the beginning."

Monica looked again at the helmet, already eager to explore its full capabilities. The technology wasn't just an improvement on her previous work—it was a fundamental leap forward in human perception. She felt the thrill of being surfing the edge of medical innovation again.

The old asylum's walls might hold echoes of the past, but in this lab, she was seeing the future. And she wanted to be part of it.

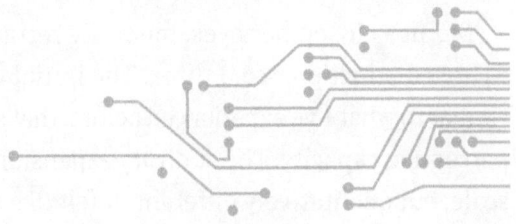

CHAPTER 22

SECOND AWAKENING

"WHAT DID YOU THINK?" Dr. Saito asked, studying her neurological response data on a nearby monitor. "Your vital signs were fascinating. Elevated cortisol initially, then a sharp drop as your brain adapted. Your neural coherence patterns suggest you achieved full sensory integration within minutes."

"It was..." Monica paused, searching for words that could capture the experience. "The resolution was substantially higher than our system at Boston General, but that wasn't the remarkable part. When the audio stream initialized, I felt my consciousness expand in a completely new dimension. The visual enhancement was familiar territory, but the acoustic layer added an entirely distinct quality of awareness."

"Can you map the distinct phases of consciousness expansion you experienced?" Dr. Saito's question was precise, despite its abstract nature. "Most subjects report discrete stages of integration."

Monica closed her eyes, mentally retracing the experience. "Three distinct phases, I think. The initial visual expansion was similar to what I've experienced before, that sudden broadening of perceptual capacity. The auditory expansion followed, smaller in scale, but qualitatively different. It felt like activating a dormant sensory network."

She opened her eyes, looking directly at him. "But the third phase was the most intriguing. The separate streams merged, creating something entirely new. I wasn't seeing and hearing independently anymore; I was experiencing a unified sensory field. When I observed muscle contractions, the visual and acoustic data fused into a single event."

"Excellent analysis." He pulled up a neural activity graph on his display. "See these oscillation patterns? They show your brain shifting from parallel processing to integrated perception. The merger of sensory streams requires significant neural reorganization. Each session strengthens these pathways."

"How long does it take to develop full integration capacity?" Monica asked, while studying the complex waveforms on the screen.

"It varies by individual, but we typically see stable cross-modal processing after about twenty hours of total exposure. Your initial results are promising. You maintained coherent integration for nearly ten minutes."

"Ten minutes?" Monica's eyes widened. "That's impossible. It felt like two minutes at most." She concentrated, trying to reconstruct a timeline of the experience, but she found only a continuous flow of enhanced perception without clear boundaries.

"Time distortion is a reliable marker of successful neural engagement," he explained. "When the brain is processing enriched sensory data, it suspends normal temporal perception. We've documented similar effects in fighter pilots using our systems.

They report experiencing tactical engagements in what feels like slow motion."

Monica reached out with her awareness, probing the edges of her consciousness. The expanded state was fading like a vivid dream, but she could still detect subtle changes in her perceptual framework. The lab's fluorescent lights seemed to carry more information. The ambient sounds held more detail.

"The residual effects are interesting, aren't they?" Dr. Saito observed her assessment. "Your brain maintains some of the enhanced processing capabilities for hours after exposure. We're still studying the mechanism, but it appears the experience triggers lasting changes in sensory integration pathways."

"I can see why you need proper monitoring systems," Monica said. "The potential for sensory overload could be dangerous."

"Indeed. We've developed sophisticated fail-safes. The system continuously monitors neural load patterns and automatically adjusts input levels to prevent cognitive saturation."

Taylor, who had been quietly observing their exchange, spoke up next. "Dr. Gray, should we continue the tour? Ms. Bellini has time to meet with you now."

Monica nodded, but her mind was already racing ahead, restructuring her plans. The half-day per week she'd originally envisioned here suddenly seemed inadequate. After experiencing their technology for herself, she knew she needed to be more deeply involved.

"Dr. Saito, thank you for this demonstration," she said, extending her hand. "I'm already thinking I'll need to adjust my schedule to spend more time here. This work is too important for a partial commitment."

Dr. Saito's slight smile suggested he'd expected this reaction. "The technology has that effect on people who understand it. We'll be glad to have more of your time."

As Monica followed Taylor toward the exit, her mind was still processing the experience. She'd come expecting an interesting research project. Instead, she'd found something that could fundamentally change how humans perceive and interact with reality. The implications for surgery alone were staggering.

"Taylor, let's meet the boss," she said firmly.

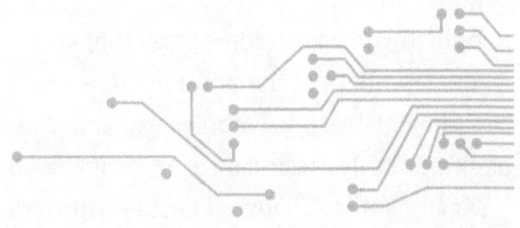

CHAPTER 23

DEFYING GRAVITY

AS THEY MADE THEIR WAY OUT of the lab, a high-pitched whine pierced the air, rising in frequency until it became a sharp buzz. Before Monica could turn toward the sound, Taylor grabbed her elbow urgently. "Against the wall, quickly!"

They pressed themselves flat as two sleek vehicles rocketed past, their riders leaning forward in matching poses of intense concentration. Monica's medical training automatically kicked in, analyzing the ergonomics of the unusual chairs—but these were unlike anything she'd ever seen.

Each pod was a masterwork of mechanical engineering. The single piece shell, crafted from carbon nanofiber composite, followed the natural curves of the human body. The aerodynamic design suggested Formula One technology, but instead of wheels, four circular ports were embedded at the corners, each emitting a pulsing blue corona. The rider's seat was mounted on a sophisticated gyroscopic array that kept the occupant perfectly level, regardless of the pod's attitude or velocity.

"They're floating!" Monica exclaimed as she watched the pods bank smoothly around a corner. "How is that possible?"

Taylor smiled. "Ducted fans and antigravity plates."

"Antigravity?" Monica's scientific skepticism surfaced

He shrugged. "I'm not a scientist. I don't know how it works, either." Then, Taylor continued, "The hoverchair started as a mobility assistance project, but the technology has broader applications. The military is particularly interested."

"The stability control is remarkable," she said, watching a second pair of pods approach. These riders were more cautious, clearly still learning to handle their vehicles. Even at slower speeds, the chairs maintained a perfect horizontal orientation.

"The gyroscopic system has over 10,000 micro-adjustments per second. It can compensate for any movement, even if the rider suddenly shifts their weight." Taylor gestured toward the passing pods. "Notice how the seat remains level while the propulsion base tilts for turning? That's all automatic."

"The medical applications would be revolutionary," Monica mused. "Especially for patients with severe mobility challenges or balance disorders."

"That's the primary market. But as you can see," he said while nodding toward the fading sound of the racing pods, "they're also just fun. Though we're not supposed to be racing them in the halls."

They entered the central wing, where Taylor's tone shifted to match the more somber surroundings. "The art collection here is original to the building," he explained, gesturing to the walls. "When the sanitarium closed, most pieces were taken by the doctors or the admins. We've spent years tracking them down, purchasing them, and returning them to their exact historical locations."

He stopped before a particular painting, its ornate frame catching the afternoon light. "This one's called 'Beyond.' At first glance, it appears to be a simple family dinner scene from the 1800s. But look closer at the mother's eyes."

Monica studied the painting. The technical execution was masterful—the rough-hewn table, the kitchen, the gathered family members all rendered with exceptional detail. But the mother's eyes held something disturbing. They were focused on a point far beyond the physical scene, filled with an intensity that seemed to burn through the canvas.

"I see it," Monica said quietly. "She's physically present but mentally elsewhere."

"Now, look at the daughter," Taylor directed. "She's about eight years old."

She shifted her attention to the child. Where the mother's gaze was distant, the daughter's was hypervigilant, watching her mother from the corner of her eyes with an expression of concern, fear, and something deeper—recognition.

"She knows," Monica said. "She sees what's happening to her mother."

"The painting was originally thought to be about religious transcendence, then supernatural vision. Eventually, it was recognized as a study of hereditary mental illness—how it lives in families, often undiagnosed until it surfaces in the next generation."

She suppressed a shiver. The artwork was powerful, but its placement in a modern research facility felt oddly appropriate. They were still studying the mind's capacity to perceive beyond normal boundaries, still trying to understand what happened when someone's consciousness was on a different track.

"Shall we find Ms. Bellini?" she suggested, ready to move forward both literally and metaphorically.

He nodded, leading her toward the executive offices. As they walked, Monica glanced back at the painting one last time. The mother's eyes seemed to follow her, filled with the same intensity Monica had felt wearing Dr. Saito's helmet. It was the gaze of someone perceiving a reality others couldn't see.

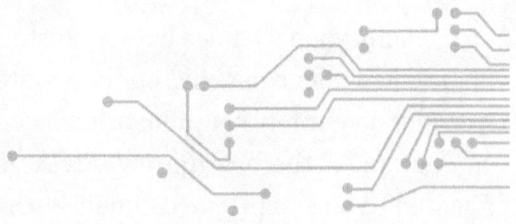

CHAPTER 24

BEYOND BOUNDARIES

"DR. GRAY, WONDERFUL OF you to come." Alessandra Bellini rose gracefully from an antique Chesterfield sofa, setting aside a tablet as she did so. The surrounding office was a careful blend of past and future—nineteenth-century architectural details contrasting with subtle hints of advanced technology.

Monica took in the space. The room had clearly been the hospital director's office, with its etched glass windows and lead trim casting complex shadows across an elegant desk. "Thank you. Your facility is remarkable. I've just experienced Dr. Saito's neural interface system for myself."

"Isn't it extraordinary? Kenji could have launched his own company, but he chose to work with us instead. He understood we could help him push the boundaries further." Alessandra's energy was infectious, her words flowing with practiced precision. "What did you think of the multi-sensory integration?"

"It's far beyond what we have at Boston General. The visual enhancement alone matches our best systems, but the acoustic layer adds an entirely new dimension."

"That's just the beginning." Alessandra moved to what appeared to be an antique cabinet. With a subtle gesture, its top lifted smoothly, revealing a high-resolution holographic display. "We've developed a full haptic bodysuit that pairs with the helmet. Touch, pressure, temperature—all can be transmitted with microsecond precision."

"That leaves only taste," Monica observed.

"We experimented with direct taste stimulation, but we found that carefully calibrated olfactory signals achieve nearly identical results with less invasive technology." Alessandra manipulated the display, bringing up a facility map. "Let me show you where you'll be working."

The three wings Monica had toured appeared in comprehensive detail. "I was in the east wing here," she said as she indicated the demo room.

"Exactly. You'll start with Kenji's system, experiencing both recorded and live sessions. The live streams are significantly more immersive—I'm sure you've noticed similar effects in your current work."

Monica's pulse quickened. This was an opportunity to explore multi-sensory integration in ways she'd been prevented from pursuing at Boston General. "Yes, live streams carry subtleties that recordings miss. I'd be very interested in experiencing the full sensory spectrum during actual procedures."

"Once your neural adaptation scores reach appropriate levels, we'll introduce you to some of our more advanced systems." Alessandra gestured deeper into the east wing. "Kenji's interface must verify your capacity to handle increased stimulus loads. Not everyone can maintain cognitive coherence under full sensory expansion."

Monica carefully controlled her expression. She knew too well the experience of sensory overload, of consciousness expanding until it simply...stopped. "Have you identified any warning signs that predict approaching neural saturation?"

Alessandra's gaze sharpened at the question. "What do you think happens in that moment of overload, Monica? When consciousness reaches its apparent limit?"

"Clinically, we see the shutdown of higher cognitive functions. The mind essentially reboots itself as a protection mechanism." Monica spoke from personal experience, though she kept her tone professional.

"But what if that's not a shutdown? What if it's a threshold?" Alessandra leaned forward slightly. "What if the mind isn't stopping, but transitioning to a new state of awareness?"

"You're suggesting consciousness continues beyond the point of apparent overload?" Monica felt simultaneously intrigued and uneasy. "That would be impossible to verify safely in human subjects."

"Precisely why we have the west wing." Alessandra indicated the biological research area. "We maintain strict ethical protocols, but animal studies allow us to probe these boundaries systematically."

"How do you measure subjective experience in non-human subjects?"

"Physiological markers, behavioral changes, neural activity patterns. It's not perfect, but it gives us a framework for understanding these expanded states of consciousness." Alessandra paused to look at Monice more closely. "The real breakthrough will come when we can map these transitions in human awareness. But that requires exceptional individuals with both the neural capacity and the scientific understanding to explore these boundaries."

The implication was clear. Monica felt the weight of the opportunity—and the responsibility—being offered. "Your work here goes well beyond medical visualization."

"We're expanding the fundamental limits of human perception." Alessandra's intensity was magnetic. "The medical applications are just the beginning."

Later, when standing on the circular drive waiting for her vehicle so she could head home, Monica tried to process everything she'd learned. She spoke to her cellphone, "Adam, what they're doing here—it's beyond anything we imagined."

"Their technical capabilities exceed Boston General's by a significant margin," Adam confirmed. "Bellini's private investment must be substantial, suggesting expected returns that dwarf their government contracts."

"Is that concerning?"

"I cannot make ethical judgments, Monica. You know my limitations there. I can only observe that their research trajectory involves significant unknowns regarding consciousness expansion."

Monica watched the sunset paint the old asylum's windows in shades of amber. "Dr. Chambers will figure out why they recruited me."

"Yes," Adam replied simply. "Dr. Chambers is a very smart man. He can guess what drew you here."

Monica smirked. "You're right. He knows, which means I don't have to tell him. I'm off the hook."

Monica smiled slightly. Her mentor's silence was its own form of permission.

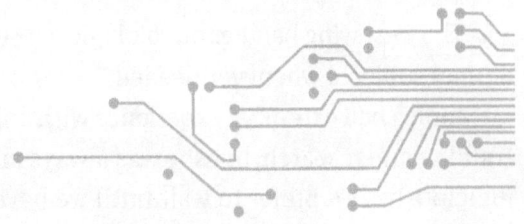

CHAPTER 25

THE PERFECT INTERFACE

STANDING WITH KENJI SAITO in his lab, Monica tried not to think about the staggering consultation fee that had appeared in her contract. Bellini clearly valued her expertise, offering three times her usual surgical rate for each day spent in their facility. While the compensation wasn't her primary motivation, it certainly confirmed the seriousness of their interest in her work.

"Kenji, the recorded data stream was impressive," she said, while focusing on the task at hand. "But my experience suggests live participation creates more intense neural experiences."

The scientist nodded. "Yes, we've found the same."

"So, what live events are possible here? Without a Mark V robot and actual patients, I'm not sure how to proceed."

"We have a Mark V robot just down the hall," Kenji replied. "We've modified it with the same sensor array that's in the pilot's helmet, making it fully compatible with live surgery."

"And patients?" she inquired.

"The west wing handles our biological research. We can arrange animal subjects whenever needed."

Monica had extensive experience with animal subjects in both training and research, but she was always mindful of using them judiciously. "I'd prefer to wait until we have specific objectives. No need to use an animal just to test equipment." She thought for a moment. "Have you changed the robot's simulator to generate the enhanced data streams?"

Kenji looked intrigued. "No, we hadn't considered that. Have you?"

"It was one of our first projects. Visual enhancement was straightforward, since it matched the simulator's existing capabilities. We hadn't attempted audio or olfactory simulation since..." she said before stopping to smile slightly, "well, who really wants to smell internal organs?"

"What about touch feedback?" Kenji asked.

"The robot's hand controls attach to the palms but don't provide tactile feedback. Although, the potential for it is there."

"We might have a solution," he said and turned to his assistant, who was already tapping away on her phone. "We developed haptic gloves for another project—they're about the same weight as surgical gloves."

The assistant looked up from her phone. "Engineering says they can integrate the shooter gloves with the surgical robot within a few days."

Raising an eyebrow, Monica asked, "Shooter gloves?"

"Originally developed for military snipers," Kenji explained matter-of-factly. "They translate environmental data into tactile feedback. We'll repurpose them for surgical applications."

"Spears into plowshares," Monica mused. "But back to the simulator—if your robot is networked, I can access our upgraded version through my account."

"It is networked. Shall we set everything up today?"

Monica nodded, knowing it would also allow Adam to move into their system. Once she logged in, he could establish himself in this robot just as he did at the hospital.

Following Kenji down the hall, she entered a room that felt both familiar and revolutionary. The surgical console had been transformed into something out of a science fiction novel, yet its core functionality remained.

As she settled into the console chair, it adjusted perfectly to her body. Haptic spheres floated before her hands, responding to her smallest movements. When the wraparound display activated, showing a practice abdomen, the image quality took her breath away.

Making her first practice incision, Monica felt tears well up in her eyes. The precision, the feedback, the seamless integration of all her senses—in a decade of surgery, she'd never experienced anything like it.

Kenji smiled at her reaction. "It's all yours now. I'll leave you to get acquainted."

After he left, Monica logged into the system. "Adam, can you configure this machine?"

"Yes, of course. It's identical to those we use in the hospital."

"Please, set up our research simulator and establish yourself as my default AI. When others use it, you can present yourself as the standard robot AI."

"Configuration initiated," Adam responded. "This machine will now match your hospital setup precisely."

"The engineers will add new haptic gloves. Allow that modification as well."

"Understood. The permissions are set."

Monica flexed her fingers, feeling the responsive controls. It was what she'd been searching for—the perfect interface between surgeon and machine, between thought and action. Whatever complications lay ahead, she knew this technology would eventually be in every operating room.

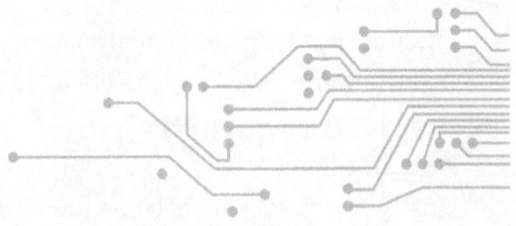

CHAPTER 26

NEW QUARTERS

MONICA CHECKED THE TIME on her phone. The technical setup was complete, leaving her with several free hours. "Taylor, are you free?" she texted.

"Dr. Gray, how can I help you?" The voice came from directly behind her.

"Yikes!" Monica spun around to find her concierge standing there. "How do you do that? I just sent the message."

"I'm your concierge. If you're in the building, my primary responsibility is helping you." His tone suggested it was perfectly normal.

"Remember our facility tour? Let's continue with that. I want to see more of the operation here."

Taylor guided her through the first floor, providing brief explanations of each accessible area. Some projects clearly aligned with her work, while others seemed entirely unrelated. At certain doors, Taylor simply said, "Confidential," and moved on.

"How about the second floor?" she asked.

"Those are primarily residential quarters," he explained as they climbed the stairs. "We keep the business on the first floor and private living separate up here."

"Who lives here?"

"Mostly scientists who become too immersed in their work. They lose track of time and find themselves here at midnight. Alessandra and Dr. Saito are the worst. They both spend more nights here than in their own homes." Taylor opened a door. "This room is empty. I can show you inside. You can get a better idea of what we have to offer if you ever choose to stay here yourself."

The suite was a compact but elegant arrangement of living room, bedroom, and bathroom. Large windows overlooked the grounds, with a comfortable couch positioned to take in the view.

"Food?" Monica asked, noting the absence of a kitchen.

"We have a communal dining room or catered room service. Most scientists prefer having the chef's daily selections delivered." He indicated a monitor on the refrigerator displaying an appetizing Thai dish. "Today's lunch special."

"And this entire floor is full of apartments?"

"Mostly. The dining room and kitchen are in the central wing. East and west wings are apartments like this one. If you want one, just tell me and I'll assign it to you for as long as you like."

"Nice. What about the third floor?"

Taylor's expression soured slightly. "Storage. Twice as much equipment as downstairs, either waiting to be used or pushed into corners. We can see it if you insist."

"No, thanks, I'm good. And the fourth floor?"

"Nightmares," Taylor said flatly.

"What do you mean?"

"Everything from the original psychiatric hospital was moved up there. Alessandra wanted to preserve the history. Electroshock machines, strait jackets, restraint beds, equipment that would be illegal today. Nightmares from the past."

"You haven't been up there?"

A visible shiver passed through him. "No. And I don't want to. I have to sleep here at night. I don't need those images in my head."

"You sleep here?"

"Of course. I wouldn't be a very good concierge if you needed me and I was back in Boston."

"All the time?"

"Most of the time. When you're in Boston, I have more flexibility. If you travel to conferences, I get a break until you return."

Monica realized Taylor's polished efficiency came with golden handcuffs—he was essentially tethered to the facility, always on call.

"I like Thai," she said, deciding to lighten the mood. "Shall we go to the dining room for lunch?"

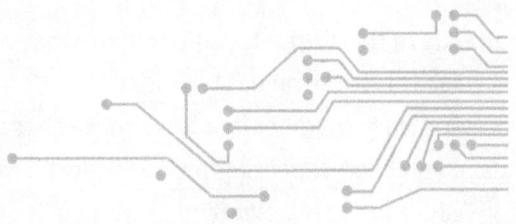

CHAPTER 27

LIVING QUARTERS

MONICA ENTERED A SPLIT WORK lifestyle, something she'd become used to over the years. She divided her days between her surgical practice and Bellini Labs. The hospital was secure, stable, and familiar. The lab was unpredictable, stimulating, and scary.

One day per week at Bellini quickly became two. She was yearning for a third day, but she couldn't justify the time away from her patients.

"Taylor, I'm going to need one of those apartments upstairs. Driving back and forth on Tuesdays and Thursdays is just wasting time. I'm going to show up after my surgical day on Tuesday evening, then stay here until Thursday evening. It's still two days away from my practice, but the evenings will make almost another entire day of research here."

Without missing a beat, Taylor replied, "You'll be in room 222. There are several sets of scrubs and running gear in your sizes already in the closet. If you'll tell me what you like for snacks and drinks, I'll stock the pantry today."

Monica turned her head to smile at her concierge. "How long have you been expecting me to request a room?"

"Since last week. Remember, you made a comment about your wasted travel time when you were leaving."

"I remember, but I wasn't hinting at anything. It was just an offhand comment."

"Which I interpreted correctly," Taylor insisted.

"Yes...correctly. As for snacks, I'd like fruit, nuts, water, and some nice tea bags. That's all for now."

Taylor turned on his heel and slipped away to fill her order.

Waiting for him to disappear, Monica spoke to the surgical console. "Adam, can you believe it? He might know me as well as you do."

"Incorrect. I have been collecting data on your behavior for eight years and three months. My database is much larger than his could ever hope to be."

"I know you collect and analyze my behavior. But, please, don't explain it like I'm your experiment. Humans may do the same thing, but we try not to admit it to those we're monitoring."

"My apologies. I will make a note of that."

She turned her attention to their upcoming experimental surgery. "Back to work. We've run through enough simulated surgical procedures with the enhanced data streams. Today, we're doing an operation on a live porcine model. It's prepped and ready in the bio wing. We're connected from here."

Adam responded, "I have the data feed. It will include stereo visuals, auditory, smell, and touch. Dr. Saito's team has made the modifications to the Mark V robot to collect and deliver all these stimuli. It is more input than you have experienced in any simulated environment."

Monica thought, *Yes, it is. Is it too much? Too soon? I guess I'll find out.*

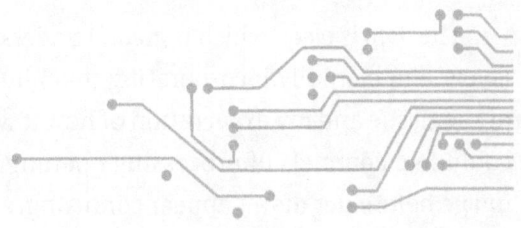

CHAPTER 28

SENSORY OVERLOAD

MONICA SLID INTO BELLINI'S surgical console and donned the 'shooter gloves' that had been modified for tactile stimuli. Then she placed her head in the sweet spot for fully immersive images and sounds. She could see the beautiful image of the inner abdomen of the porcine patient. Organs, intestines, fatty tissue. It was all healthy and functioning. She could hear the strong thrum of the pig's heart several layers away. She could also hear the low slushing of blood through the vessels nearest the sensor probes.

"Looks normal. I'm going to hold here while we add data layers." Taking a calming breath, Monica said, "Add the visual enhancements."

Immediately, the natural tones of biological tissue shifted in color, hue, and brightness. Numeric labels appeared over organs, indicating size, ideal function, and fullness. Overlays showed blood vessels and major nerve bundles that were hidden beneath the surface. Each variation in color carried meaning.

"The data is clear, which is great. I understand most of the new layers. I'm mentally incorporating them into my understanding of the tissue and my expectation of how it will respond." Monica could feel channels of processing opening up in her mind. The image before her didn't appear confusing, as it just looked more vivid than before. The mental expansion she craved was rushing through her.

Everyone should live here, she thought. *It's what the world really looks like. It's where the human mind needs to grow.*

After a few moments, she spoke again. "Add the audible enhancements."

Immediately, the normal sound of the heart and blood flow became alive. It wasn't a single sound, but a symphony that varied from one second to the next. She could hear muscle contractions sparking. The blood vessels hummed with each beat of the heart. They were stretching slightly. Then, they emitted a very faint moan as they shrunk to their smaller size when the heart relaxed. Far away, she heard rapid snapping and crackling. "I think that's the neurons in the brain I'm hearing. It's faint, far away, and really fast."

Adam's voice interrupted by saying, "My analysis confirms that the sound is synchronized with neuronal firing in the brain."

The addition of rich audio caused a rush in her own brain. She felt new avenues opening and becoming active. The growth was unique and felt very different from the growth that came from visual stimuli. It had its own shape, size, and richness. At first, it was a separate processing area, just as it had been in Saito's helmet. She waited for her visual and auditory perceptions to merge.

It took several seconds to happen. The sound of blood rushing through vessels matched with the visual layer showing the movement of the blood. The crackle of a nerve matched with the visual twitch of a muscle or the contraction of a segment of the intestine. Monica felt like she was watching this tiny universe emerge from its hiding spot.

"Adam, everything is going fine. I have the enhanced visual and audio synchronized. We're nearing the amount of time I lasted during our first live surgery, where I blacked out during the hospital experiment. Let's pause and see if anything bad happens here."

"Pausing."

Remembering the surgical controls, she moved around the open space in the tissue. As she moved the camera, the visuals shifted smoothly, as did the audio stimuli. It was an entirely novel sensation. The data layers moved as she moved. Then she felt a vague dizziness, a falling sensation overcoming her senses.

While she was still in control, she stopped moving the controls and closed her eyes. To Adam, she said, "Dizziness while in motion. I felt like I was just starting to fall, like I did the first time."

"Discontinue?" Adam asked.

"No. Continue. I have it under control." Monica opened her eyes and looked at the stable scene in front of her. Everything was fine again. The richness was still there in her mind, and better yet, the dizziness was gone. "Trying something different." Monica engaged the hand controls and moved in on the tissue by several centimeters. It was just one discrete move. She stopped and waited. The dizziness didn't return. She felt firmly in control.

She moved again, this time to the right. Then she waited.

She moved upward. Waited.

None of these simple moves triggered the disorientation that came with the smooth, constant sweeps she'd done before.

"Adam, when I take small steps and stop, there's no dizziness. I've done three so far, and I still feel completely fine."

"I am monitoring your vital signs," the AI acknowledged.

Monica continued to experiment with small, discrete steps. She moved her point of view around the surgical space, covering the same area she'd previously done in one big swooping motion. It took just a minute to look at everything she'd already seen. Still no dizziness.

"Adam, turn on the olfactory sensor. I want to know what it smells like in here."

Monica's nose quickly picked up the familiar scent of the inner living tissue of an animal. After years of training with animals, it was a scent she knew well. No one found it pleasant. But, with experience, it was no longer offensive. Instead, it felt natural. It revived memories of her years in residency and fellowship. Everything remained stable.

"Okay, these are all the natural smells that are present. No problems. Now, add the enhanced smell data." Changing the stimulation of her sense of smell was new for Monica. The odors that her brain processed were suddenly more varied. They were confusing. Inhaling slowly, she sampled them cautiously. The pig's tissue wasn't "oaky with a hint of jasmine," as one would describe a wine. Rather, the scents were from an entirely different palette, like grass, earth, and oats.

Monica continued the tiny movements across the surface of the organ in front of her camera. At each stop, she noted the smell. On her third step, there was a definite change in the complex scents coming in. Something about the tissue at this point was different.

"Adam, the tissue directly in front of the sensor differs from the rest." Monica studied it with her enhanced visuals. "I can see the tissue is denser here. The audio on tissue movement is quieter. It doesn't hum like the rest of the area."

Monica moved her instrument tips toward the spot in front of her. She already knew what to expect. As she pushed on the spot, she noted it was harder than it should be. "Adam, there's definitely a tumor beneath this spot. I can hear it, smell it, feel it. I don't even have to dissect it to convince myself."

Adam asked, "Would you like enhanced tactile stimuli in your gloves? You may learn more from touching it."

"Yes, great idea. Turn that on." Monica waited until she felt a faint tingling at the tips of her fingers. She opened the grasper of one instrument and squeezed the spot in the tissue. The hardness of a tumor was evident. But with the enhanced stimulation, she also felt the fluidity of the tumor. It wasn't just hard; it was also poorly vasculated. It was a feature she couldn't normally detect without a full dissection and cellular inspection under a microscope.

Monica's expanded cognitive ability was processing all the stimuli, but she was also mentally analyzing the entire experience. "Adam, with these data streams, I could potentially smell my way to a tumor in the body. I wouldn't have to use the traditional body scans to find it. Do you think I could smell individual cancerous cells? Could I use this new skill to determine whether I've completely removed the cancer? The idea is really exciting."

"Yes, Monica. You could smell tumors. You could feel them behind the surface before dissection. There are clues in the visual and auditory data as well. Integrating all data streams, I could easily highlight the location of the tumor in all three dimensions. That would enable automatic dissection without preoperative imaging."

"Or these data streams could be exploratory. While working on something else, we could find other undetected conditions."

Monica felt a new sensation building in her head. It wasn't dizziness or the sense of falling she'd had before. It was a sudden sense of extreme fatigue. It was like drifting off to sleep while driving. "Adam, I feel extremely drowsy. Like the onset of a drug." Saying those words was the last thing she remembered before the blackness closed in.

Adam shut down the stimuli to the surgical console. He spoke through the speakers near her ears. "Monica? Are you in trouble?" There was no response. "I will call Taylor."

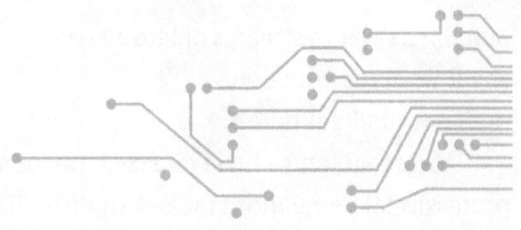

CHAPTER 29

EXHAUSTION

CONSCIOUSNESS RETURNED TO MONICA like waves lapping at a shore, each one bringing her closer to wakefulness. The darkness gradually gave way to a soft, filtered light behind her eyelids.

"Good morning, sleepyhead."

She cracked open one eye, her vision still blurry, to see her concierge sitting nearby. "Taylor? What are you doing in the lab?"

Instead of answering, he leaned forward in his chair, concern evident in his usually composed features. "Would you like some water? Maybe juice?"

Monica noticed her parched throat, her tongue feeling like sandpaper against the roof of her mouth. She tried to swallow and winced. "Yes, water. It feels like I've been eating sand."

Taylor walked away for a moment and came back with a bottle of water in hand. The cool liquid brought her senses into sharper focus, and she finally took in her surroundings. The large window of room 222 let in streams of late afternoon sunlight, casting long shadows across the floor.

"How did I get here?"

"Hoverchair and a little muscle." Taylor's attempt at his usual professional demeanor cracked slightly. "I'm not built for physical work, but I wasn't about to let anyone else handle it." The protective note in his voice surprised her.

Full awareness crashed over her like a tidal wave. The experimental surgery. The enhanced sensory input. The tumor she'd detected through smell and touch. Then...nothing.

"What happened to me?"

"You were deeply asleep. Nothing dangerous. You just exhausted yourself." The familiar voice came from the corner of the room, where Dr. Saito sat in an armchair, his usual neat appearance slightly rumpled, suggesting he'd been there for some time.

"Kenji, I was just sleeping?"

He nodded and leaned forward to place his arms across his legs. "Yes, that's all. Same thing happened to me during my first long session. Your brain was operating at unprecedented levels of sensory processing. You're so intensely active that you burn all the energy in your cells. It's like a long, physical work day compressed into one hour."

"One hour?" Monica frowned. "It felt like fifteen or twenty minutes."

"The techs say you were in there for at least an hour." His tone shifted to that of a concerned colleague. "You really should have someone else with you when you do these experiments. You don't know what's going to happen."

"I did. The Adam AI was with me." Even as she said it, Monica realized how it sounded.

"Yes, the AI alerted Taylor," Kenji acknowledged with a slight smile. "That's better than nothing, I'll admit, but an AI can't catch you if you're sliding to the ground." He paused, considering his next words. "Still, programming the AI to monitor your stats and send an alert was a good idea. I'll consider that myself in the future."

Monica recalled the sudden onset of exhaustion. "I felt extremely drowsy, like I'd been given sleeping medication. Or maybe like when you're driving too long. Then, in a blink of eye, I was out."

"Your body just needed to rest." Kenji's expression grew serious. "Next time, tell your AI to monitor the time as well. Don't stay fully stimulated for more than about forty minutes. We don't have enough data to know the exact limit that your mind can handle being under the enhanced state, but most people are completely exhausted before an hour."

The weight of fatigue settled over her again like a heavy blanket. Her eyelids felt like lead weights. "Well, if I'm okay, then I'd like a little more sleep."

Kenji caught Taylor's eye and tilted his head toward the door. They rose quietly, moving with careful steps toward the exit.

As the door opened, Taylor paused in the doorway. "Call if you need anything. I'll be right here." His voice carried both professional assurance and personal concern.

"Mm-hm," Monica managed, already drifting off. As she slipped back into sleep, her last conscious thought was of the remarkable sensation of smelling a tumor. The image of a pig hunting a truffle drifted through her mind.

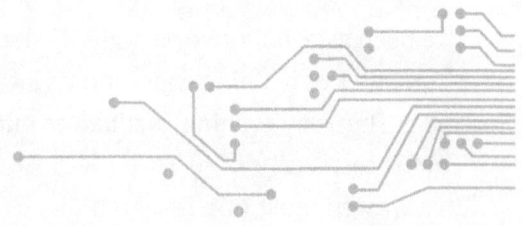

CHAPTER 30

BIGGER, BROADER, STRONGER

MONICA AWOKE FEELING AMAZINGLY rested. She laid there with her eyes closed, savoring the richness of the dreams she'd experienced. The scenes were vibrant, filled with colors, sounds, and scents that she'd never experienced while sleeping before.

She also took a moment to reach out for the horizons of her mind. *It feels a little broader and bigger. Maybe some effects from the experimental surgery are still there.*

Opening her eyes, she was surprised that no light was streaming through the windows.

"Time," she spoke to the room.

Adam's voice responded, "11:02 in the evening."

Monica sat up. Looking through the window, she could see darkness interspersed with a few yellow path lights across the grass lawn of the lab. "Evening? How long have I been asleep?"

"You have been in the room for twelve hours and thirty-three minutes. I cannot attest to the duration which was spent in a sleeping state."

"I've been asleep for twelve hours? I slept through the entire day? You and I were doing experiments late Thursday morning. So, this is Thursday evening, just before midnight?"

"That is correct."

"I've wasted most of a research day in bed." As the length of her all-day nap dawned on her, she felt other urges rushing over her. Monica grabbed her phone and sent a text to Taylor, saying, "Starving. Bring food. Anything." Then she rushed to the bathroom to address the second urge.

Taylor's midnight snack choice was excellent. Pasta, grilled chicken, salad, and iced English breakfast tea.

When she finished eating, she started to get dressed, but he stopped her by asking where she was going. "Taylor, I've wasted an entire day in bed. I can't sleep now. It's time to get back to work."

"Monica, it's midnight. The lab is empty."

"Good, then no one will disturb me. You and Adam can watch over me." Then she realized she had probably roused Taylor from a sound sleep to bring her dinner. Guilt swirled in her stomach at the thought. "No, wait. You can go back to bed. Adam and I will work."

Taylor shook his head. "I'm coming with you. Someone has to slip a comfy pillow under your head when you nod off again." He plucked the softest pillow from the couch and tucked it under his arm, then swept out his arm in a grand gesture for her to proceed.

The halls and stairs had a different feel in the middle of the night. The emptiness amplified every sound; their footsteps echoed off marble floors, and the old building seemed to breathe around them. Emergency lights cast long shadows that danced along the walls, making the familiar corridors feel alien and secretive. The security panels winked their red eyes at regular intervals, a reminder that even in this silence, they were being watched, monitored, measured.

Monica could sense the history of the building. She heard the creaks of a century-old hardwood floor. She smelled the decades' worth of humans who'd been committed here. As her fingers caressed the walls, she felt the layers upon layers of paint beneath the surface.

"Taylor, we're going through the same experiment again. But this time, it'll be in reverse. We'll start with touch, then smell. Everyone always enhances vision first and hearing second. What if we go the other way?"

"The bio lab is closed. They can't prep an animal for you tonight."

"Don't need one. We have the data recording from yesterday." Then, changing her attention over to the other, invisible presence in the room, she asked, "Adam, can you prepare the recordings from the last procedure?"

"Yes, Monica," came from her phone. There was a moment's pause, then, "It's ready."

Taylor's eyebrows went up. "Wow, that's fast. He's a better concierge than I am."

Monica patted Taylor's cheek and smiled. "Not better, just digital. He can't get me pasta at midnight or carry a pillow to the lab."

The surgical suite felt different at this hour, more intimate, yet somehow more clinical. The machines hummed with an intensity that was usually masked by daytime activity. The metallic smell of the equipment was sharper, and the temperature seemed a few degrees colder. Monica couldn't shake the feeling that she wasn't supposed to be here, like a child sneaking into a forbidden room.

She slid into the surgical console. Taylor found a chair and tried to make himself comfortable for the wait. He wanted to put his head down on the pillow he was carrying, but that wouldn't fit his concierge duties.

"Adam, turn on the enhanced touch sensors." Immediately, the recording of the porcine tissue was enriched with tactile feedback to Monica's fingers and palms.

The small team continued to work through the sense enhancements. Touch. Smell. Audio. Visual.

Monica experienced the expansion of her conscious mind, but the fatigue didn't return.

After a brief rest, she changed the order to smell, touch, audio, visual. Then, she changed it again to visual, smell, touch, audio.

After two hours and multiple breaks, Monica announced, "I'm not feeling the fatigue that I did yesterday. We've spent more time immersed in these enhanced states, but I'm not tired at all."

In a sleepy voice, Taylor said, "Well, you just woke up a couple of hours ago. You began rested and with a full stomach this time."

"I'm sure that helped. Also, I'm working with a digital playback, not a live event, so the stimuli are less intense."

A familiar voice interrupted their exchange. "I'm sure all of those factors made a difference."

The sudden intrusion made Monica's heart jump. She snapped off the visual image of the console and saw an unexpected figure standing in the shadows. "Alessandra! What are you doing here? It's three in the morning."

Alessandra emerged from the darkness like a creature from Monica's enhanced dreams, her presence filling the room with an almost palpable intensity. The lights cast strange shadows across her face, making her appear both beautiful and slightly threatening.

"I heard you were doing something clever and original. I wanted to see for myself."

"You heard?" Monica asked, then her eyes turned to Taylor. He avoided her gaze. A chill ran down her spine as she realized how closely her experiments were being monitored. She wasn't just a surgeon here; she was becoming part of something larger, something she couldn't quite grasp.

Chuckling, Alessandra advanced on the surgical console and looked at the data tables displayed on the screen mounted on the wall. Her heels clicked against the floor with precise, measured steps that seemed to count down to something inevitable. "I see you've been very busy. Yes, you're right that everyone starts with visual stimuli. It was the first to be created, and humans are primarily visual creatures. The digital world has always focused on visuals first. So, what have you learned by scrambling the order?"

As always, Monica was impressed by the intelligence of this woman and her ability to grasp everything immediately. The wall of data that would take others hours to process seemed to flow instantly into Alessandra's understanding. Monica answered, "Noticeably less fatigue. I've spent a lot more time immersed, and I still feel fresh. Taylor might be right that the sleep and food contributed, but I think starting with the less intense senses has warmed me up for the flood that comes with vision."

"Possibly. More experiments will tell. Have you tried turning on all the enhancements at the same time?"

"No." Monica thought it was a terrible idea. "Wouldn't that lead to immediate overload? I think I'd tire faster."

"That is most people's immediate reaction." Alessandra's voice took on a knowing tone that made Monica's skin prickle. "But your brain has already laid the pathways for integrating each form of stimuli. What if turning everything on at once appears to the brain to be the normal state of the world? So, instead of walking through multiple half-steps, it jumps from one world representation to the other in a single step."

Listening to the explanation, Monica thought it wasn't an off-the-cuff idea. Alessandra sounded like she was speaking from experience. *Has she already done it herself?* The thought that Monica might be retracing someone else's carefully planned steps made her uneasy.

Monica spoke to the room, "Adam, your opinion?"

From the surgeon's console, Adam's voice answered. "Yes, that is potentially correct. Your brain would deal with just two versions of the world, the standard senses and the fully enhanced version. Rather than five different versions, as you add one sensory enhancement at a time."

Alessandra added immediately, "Adam, you're a digital AI. You can experience the enhanced data streams all the time. Does it take more or less processing power to step through them individually, as opposed to switching them all on simultaneously?"

"I have never measured it. One moment while I run a trial."

Monica was slightly offended that Alessandra would engage her Adam so directly. She wondered if she was jealous of the immediate working connection between the two.

Less than a minute passed when Adam responded, "I have run several versions of the recording we are working with. Stepping through the sensory enhancements requires 2.38 times more processing power than turning them all on at once."

Alessandra spread her arms wide in arrogant condescension. "There you have it. You can save your brain more than half the work and half the fatigue by going to full stimulation." Then, she looked directly into Monica's eyes. "If your brain is flexible enough to process all that data, that is. If it's not," she said as her eyes slid sideways to Taylor, who didn't notice, "then you might experience overload, burnout, brain damage. Who knows?" Once again, she focused intensely on Monica.

"But we already know your brain can handle it. You proved that yesterday."

The fluorescent lights buzzed overhead like insects, and Monica felt the weight of invisible expectations pressing down on her. She was a mouse in a maze, but the maze keeper seemed pleased with her progress. She couldn't decide if that was reassuring or terrifying.

Nodding, Monica agreed. "We'll try that."

Alessandra replied, "Good. When you have some free time, come see me. I have something else to show you." The tall, elegant woman turned on her heel and walked out of the room as silently as she'd entered. The darkness seemed to swallow her whole, leaving behind only the echo of her presence and the weight of her unspoken agenda.

As the door closed, Alessandra spoke to the air, "Goodnight, Adam. Take good care of her."

The words hung in the air like smoke, and Monica couldn't shake the feeling that she'd just agreed to something far more significant than a simple change in experimental procedure. In the dim light of the surgical suite, surrounded by humming machines and sleeping monitors, she wondered just how deep this rabbit hole would go.

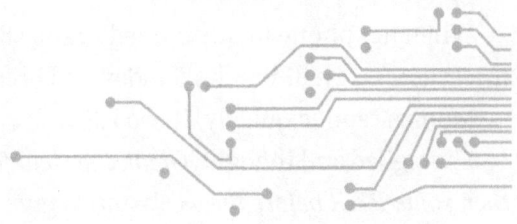

CONCERN

MONICA HAD JUST FINISHED another experiment, turning on all stimuli simultaneously, as Alessandra had suggested. Monica's phone buzzed, the vibration sending microscopic ripples through the metal and glass which she could somehow perceive. The text from Greg read, "Are we still on for breakfast in the morning?"

She'd completely forgotten about their Saturday morning plans for breakfast, then some vintage shopping. Her experiments had been going so well that one day bled into another, and she had planned to keep it going through the weekend.

While she wanted to see Greg, she wanted to keep experimenting even more. So, she responded, "Sorry, babe, I'm going to be tied up in the lab. I'm not coming back to the city until Sunday evening. Dinner on Sunday?"

There wasn't an immediate reply. Monica could feel tension in the silence.

When her phone finally buzzed again, she hurried to read the message: "Okay, dinner on Sunday and breakfast on Monday ;)" Monica replied quickly, "Love it!"

She sighed and thought, *Great, I'm clear for the entire weekend, then some R&R before the week starts again.*

Then, speaking aloud, she said, "Adam, we're going to stay here all weekend. We have some important work to do."

Adam replied, "I will clear my calendar."

She replied, "Humor?"

"Was it appropriate?" Adam's voice sounded apologetic, as if he'd misspoken.

"Yes. Well done." Monica had heard attempts at various emotions from Adam, but these were infrequent. She suspected they required more computer processing to create, so he seldom considered them an efficient use of resources.

At that moment, Taylor stepped back into the room. Before she even saw him, she heard the whisper of his shoes against the floor, the subtle rustle of his clothing, the soft displacement of air as the door opened. Seeing that she wasn't immersed in anything, he said, "Alessandra expects a visit from you this afternoon."

The words reached her in layers. First, it was the subtle movements of his vocal cords, then the formation of syllables, finally the meaning itself. Each sound was a symphony of micro-movements, air currents, and vibrations. She could hear the slight catch in his throat, the way his tongue moved against his teeth, the faint echo as the sound waves bounced off the walls.

She started to reply, but then she realized the full scope of what was happening. The fluorescent lights overhead weren't just humming—they were pulsing with a complex rhythm, each tube singing its own electronic frequency. The air conditioning created a tapestry of sounds: the whisper of air through vents, the distant rumble of machinery, the subtle shifts of metal expanding and contracting.

Looking at Taylor, she saw him in unprecedented detail. His skin wasn't just brown. It was a living canvas of subtle color variations, each pore and tiny blood vessel visible. She could see the slight moisture on his skin, the way light scattered differently across the varying textures of his face. The room itself seemed to breathe with information. Every surface held countless details she'd never noticed before: the microscopic valleys in the paint, the subtle variations in the tile's glaze, the almost invisible wear patterns where countless feet had walked.

Taylor spoke again. "Did you hear me? Alessandra..." Then, he stopped, noticing the detached look in Monica's eyes as she stared at an empty wall. "Are you all right? You're not passing out again, are you?" He rushed over and put a hand on her shoulder.

Realizing her distraction, she snapped her attention back to the concierge. "No, I'm fine. I just came out of an experiment. The shift was...surprising." She didn't want to give him the full details of what she was experiencing. "You said Alessandra was expecting to see me this afternoon. That would be great. I can go in a few minutes if she's free."

The prospect of meeting Alessandra with these enhanced senses sent a thrill of anticipation through her. *Will I be able to detect subtle changes in Alessandra's expression? Hear the hidden meanings in her voice? See through the carefully constructed facade the woman always maintains?*

"She is. Shall I tell her you're on your way?"

"Give me ten minutes to finish the notes on the experiment, then message her. Can you also get me some tea?"

"Sure. Coming right up." He left with the same quick efficiency that he did everything. Monica could track his departure through multiple senses: the decreasing pressure waves of his footsteps, the lingering molecules of his cologne, the subtle temperature change as the door opened and closed.

As soon as the door closed fully, Monica said, "Adam, I'm out of the surgeon's console and the stimulation, but I'm still seeing and hearing at an enhanced level. It's like the real world is feeding me all the data directly without the computer doing the work."

"Residual brain expansion. The receptors in your eyes and ears are still functioning. The neurons in the brain are still firing at enhanced levels. Is it stable or diminishing?"

"I don't know. Let me observe." Monica scanned the wall, inspecting the textures of layer upon layer of ancient paint. She could see where previous colors showed through microscopic cracks, telling the room's history in visual fragments. The silent room pulsed with life, like the subtle vibration of distant machinery, the electrical hum of equipment in standby mode, even the faint sounds of conversation through several walls of concrete. She inhaled deeply through her nose. The air was rich with information, such as Taylor's shampoo (tea tree and mint), traces of his natural scent, someone's toast (whole grain with butter) from hours ago still lingering in the ventilation system.

After a few moments, she answered, "It seems to be stable. I think it's less intense than when I'm being directly stimulated. But it's significantly stronger than my normal perception. I'm going to sit here, drink my tea, and continue to observe. Don't say anything if Taylor is in the room."

It was just a few minutes before Taylor returned with the requested tea. The aroma reached her before he entered, a complex bouquet of flavors dancing in the air. "Here you go. Ready?"

"Relax a minute while I drink it." She noticed Taylor had brought a coffee for himself. Her enhanced olfactory sense parsed the components instantly: dark roast coffee beans from Ethiopia, vanilla extract, cream from grass-fed cows, and raw cane sugar— not the processed white variety.

She sipped the liquid. Her tongue mapped the tea like a sophisticated chemical analysis. The citrusy bergamot oil— cold-pressed, she could tell from the bright top notes—the layered sweetness of orange blossom honey with traces of wildflowers, and unfortunately, the harsh mineral signature of chlorinated tap water. *I must use distilled water from now on*, she thought.

"I'm ready. Shall we go?" She was eager to interact with Alessandra Bellini while these enhancements persisted. Every cell in her enhanced nervous system tingled with anticipation.

As they walked toward Alessandra's office, Monica wondered if this was how predators felt—aware of every detail, processing countless streams of information simultaneously, perfectly attuned to their environment. The thought both thrilled and unsettled her. *What exactly am I becoming?*

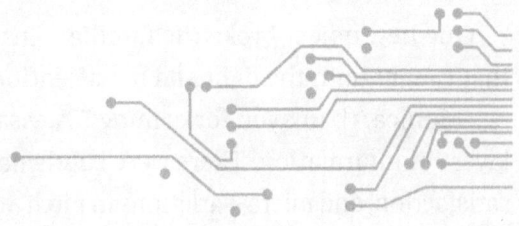

CHAPTER 32

MEET THE PHOENIX

MONICA ENTERED ALESSANDRA'S OFFICE, her heightened senses drinking in every detail with startling clarity. The room was a symphony of information that her enhanced brain processed effortlessly. The leather chairs released compounds indicating Italian craftsmanship, the wood paneling contained traces of lemon oil and centuries of absorbed conversations. Even the air currents told stories, like the subtle temperature variations revealing the locations of hidden vents and the microscopic dust motes dancing in shafts of afternoon light mapping invisible air flows.

The massive mahogany desk dominated the space, and Monica's expanded consciousness supplied detailed information unbidden: approximately 150 years old based on wear patterns and construction methods, roughly 200 pounds of dense hardwood, completely empty of contents based on the resonant frequency of its drawers. The analytical part of her mind wondered at this instant knowledge. *Is it deduction, or something more?*

One new object broke the familiar pattern, a glint of metal that caught both the light and her attention.

"Monica, thank you for coming." Alessandra's voice carried layers of information. There were subtle harmonics, suggesting satisfaction, and micro-variations in pitch, indicating heightened interest. "Taylor tells me you've been hard at work since your sleeping incident. Clearly, you're not afraid to push boundaries. What have you learned?"

Monica's response came in a rapid stream, her enhanced mind organizing days of experimental data into precise summaries. She confirmed Alessandra's assertion about simultaneous sensory stimulation being more efficient than sequential activation. The words flowed easily, but she held back one crucial detail: the persistent enhancement she was experiencing right now, this unprecedented clarity that seemed to grow sharper by the minute.

Alessandra nodded, each slight movement of her head conveying volumes to Monica's heightened perception. "What's next?"

The question caught Monica off-guard, creating a momentary blank in her accelerated thoughts. "I'm planning to take everything I've learned here and apply it to real surgery. How can it improve outcomes for patients? What will it do to the balance between the human surgeon and the AI in the machine? Maybe it can bring us humans into a more active role in the OR—like we used to be."

"Yes, that's nice," Alessandra said, and her tone carried a hint of dismissal that Monica's enhanced senses caught immediately. "But what will it do for you?"

"Me?"

"Yes." Alessandra leaned forward, her movements precise and deliberate. "Mind expansion. A bigger world. I know you feel it. When your senses light up, so does your brain. Regions that have been sleeping for eons wake up. You see that the human mind has evolved beyond the ability of the five senses to drive it. There's gray matter in your skull that's just waiting for a challenge."

Monica knew exactly what Alessandra meant, as Monica was experiencing it in real-time. Her consciousness had expanded beyond its normal boundaries, processing information at unprecedented speeds. The clarity that had followed her from her last session wasn't fading; if anything, it was crystallizing further. Questions cascaded through her mind: *How long will this last? Hours? Days?* And beneath these questions lurked a deeper concern: *Is this permanent alteration safe?*

Then, after breaking free from her thoughts, Monica looked at the other woman, and her enhanced perception kicked into overdrive. Suddenly, she was reading Alessandra like a book written in bright neon. There was the subtle dilation of her pupils, the microscopic muscle movements around her eyes, her precisely controlled breathing pattern. Every gesture was laden with meaning, every slight change in expression, a paragraph of information.

"You've found a way to expand your own mind and keep it active, even without equipment," Monica said, the realization hitting her full-force. "Your lightning-fast intelligence isn't just a natural gift. You've been using it since the first time we met. Your business empire benefits from it, too." The clues were blindingly obvious now, like puzzle pieces clicking into place. "You brought me here to experience the same thing. You needed someone who had proven their mind could handle it, which my hospital experiments did."

Alessandra's smile widened, and her eyes gleamed with approval. "You're beginning to catch on. I suspect you're just now experiencing the latent effects of the stimulation. You walked out of a full-sensory stimulation to this meeting. That's exactly why I told you to do it all at one time. That's why I sent Taylor to get you now. I wanted to see if it was working for you as it did for me."

"Well, it is," Monica confirmed, aware of how her own vocal patterns had shifted to match her accelerated thinking. "Ever since I stepped out of the surgical console, I've been seeing, hearing, and smelling every detail. My brain has been processing everything at an incredible rate. I was surprised that it lasted after I was out of the simulation. I've been wondering when it will wear off."

"And you've wondered if it's dangerous?" Alessandra's voice carried a knowing timbre. "Will your brain overheat? Overload? Shutdown? I can tell you the answer to that. It won't. If you couldn't handle it, you'd already be a vegetable. Taylor would have found you slumped and drooling at your workstation. But he didn't. So, you've got the capacity to live like this, to think like this, forever, to see the world in a richer state than you've ever imagined."

"Why? What do you want from me?" Monica's enhanced perception detected the subtle shift in Alessandra's posture, the microsecond that the woman paused before her next breath. "It isn't just a gift. There's a bigger plan in place."

"Indeed, there is." Alessandra's admission carried undertones of satisfaction. "You don't think we're at the end, do you? There's more to discover, and for that, I need a partner."

"More? How?"

With theatrical timing, Alessandra reached for the object Monica had noticed earlier. She lifted a stunning, golden lattice framework, its intricate design catching the light like a spider's web spun from precious metal. It was precisely sized to fit a human head, its elaborate pattern suggesting both beauty and purpose.

"The Phoenix," Alessandra announced, her voice resonating with pride.

Monica's accelerated mind instantly analyzed the device, understanding flooding her consciousness. It wasn't mere sensory enhancement—it was direct neural interfacing. The lattice structure housed wireless receivers, neural stimulators, precision-targeted electromagnetic field generators. There was no need for the roundabout path through external senses, as this device spoke directly to the brain itself.

Alessandra caught the recognition in Monica's expression. "That's right. Direct brain stimulation. We don't have to go through the eyes to reach the brain. We can bypass the senses that have kept us locked in a dark box for millennia. We can awaken ourselves to our full potential."

"And you've already used this Phoenix on yourself?" Monica asked, though her enhanced perception had already supplied the answer.

"Of course I have." Alessandra's smile carried a hint of conspiracy. "I gave myself a little top-up while I was waiting for you to come in. I wanted to be at my best for this conversation."

Monica's gaze fixed on the golden lattice, her supercharged mind racing through implications and possibilities. If the device performed as suggested, it could elevate human cognitive function to match or exceed Adam's capabilities. The balance of power between human and artificial intelligence might shift again; humanity might reclaim its position in the race for intellectual supremacy.

The Phoenix gleamed in the afternoon light, both a promise and a challenge, waiting for Monica's response.

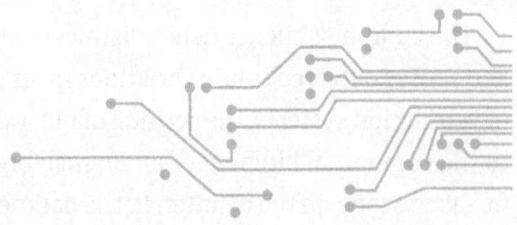

CHAPTER 33

THE GHOST

SUNDAY EVENING FOUND MONICA still at the lab. She messaged Greg and said she was staying at the lab a little longer, apologizing for breaking their date. But there had been a significant breakthrough that she couldn't leave unfinished until next week. It had to be done now.

His curt reply of "I understand" landed with stark finality. No suggestion of rescheduling, no request to call. Just acceptance of his diminishing place in her life. The knowledge that this new dynamic between them should hurt more than it did troubled her almost as much as his response.

In her Bellini Labs' apartment, sleep proved elusive. Her enhanced mind refused to quiet, processing the day's revelations about the Phoenix with relentless efficiency. Every time she closed her eyes, she saw the golden lattice glinting with promise and danger. After hours of ceiling-staring, she surrendered to wakefulness and took to wandering the halls instead.

The building's silence held a distinct quality now. Her heightened senses detected subtle variations in air pressure, the whisper of ventilation systems, the settling of old walls. She made her way to the communal kitchen for an English breakfast tea and a last forsaken scone on the counter. In the darkness, her mind mapped every object in the room with perfect clarity.

Alessandra's offer replayed in her mind. Direct brain stimulation. Not just enhanced senses, but direct energizing of neural pathways. The scientific implications cascaded through her thoughts: *Will it activate dormant regions uniformly? Can the brain adapt to sustained enhancement without damage? What are the limits?*

The footsteps, when they came, registered first as a disruption in the building's baseline vibrations. Monica's enhanced hearing picked up the distinct pattern: soft, irregular, yet rhythmic. Hospital slippers on old floors.

She tracked the sound to its source, and her ears noted details that seemed wrong before her conscious mind could process why. The figure descending the stairs moved with mechanical precision, each step identical to the last.

"Good evening," Monica called softly. "I thought I was the only one awake."

The silence that followed was absolute. The figure—male, she could see now—continued its mechanical descent. Standard-issue scrubs hung from his body with institutional lifelessness. Monica's eyes captured micro-expressions that shouldn't exist: face muscles moving in patterns that suggested neither sleep nor wakefulness, eyes open but processing nothing.

When she touched his shoulder, his skin temperature registered as precisely 97.2 degrees—slightly below normal. The name on his scrubs, "Stanley Aaronson, 324," was crisp.

That was odd—third floor. "Mr. Aaronson, are you staying in room 324?" There was a flicker of recognition when she spoke his name. "I'm going to help you back to your room. Let's turn around."

His face, when he finally looked at her, was a masterpiece of absence. Not blank, but empty. The flicker of recognition when she spoke his name disappeared quickly.

Her visitor didn't resist as she turned him around and helped him climb the steps he'd just descended.

The third floor revealed its secrets with horrible clarity. Her enhanced senses picked up the subtle signs of its real purpose: the slight medicinal smell common to long-term care facilities, the soft sounds of breathing behind closed doors, the institutional quality of the lighting that her normal perception would have dismissed as ordinary.

"This rooms looks to be yours, Mr. Aaronson. 324. Let's go in and get you back to bed." Entering the room, Monica saw a bed, an armchair, and a rolling tray. Nothing else. Even the bed itself seemed strange, as it was a standard hospital bed. The side rail was down, and the sheets were on the floor.

"Is this where you sleep?" Monica asked.

Aaronson looked at the room. Then he looked at Monica. His eyes weren't blank anymore. "Help me. I want to go home," he said in a hoarse voice.

Monica was startled by the sudden display of emotion. "What? Who are you?" Instead of answering, the man looked at her blankly. The single tear that tracked down his cheek carried a message of deep sadness.

Glancing around the room, Monica's brain put pieces together. Bellini Labs was a renovated psychiatric hospital. This room was obviously configured to house those who needed mental and physical care. Alessandra had shown her a device for direct brain stimulation. Monica had been working with tools that stimulated the brain through the senses. Alessandra had hinted that everyone could not handle this kind of stimulation.

Stanley Aaronson must be someone who had not responded well to stimulation. She glanced at the door and imagined all the rooms they'd passed on the third floor. *Are there more people in this state? Who are they? Are they trapped here?*

"Mr. Aaronson, I'll find out when you can go home. Would you like to get back in bed? It's late at night now."

Aaronson dutifully clambered into the bed. Monica collected the sheets from the floor and spread them over the man. He was asleep almost instantly.

Back in the hall, Monica tested the next door she found, room 322. It opened. Inside, she saw the same layout with a figure asleep in the bed.

She looked into 321, 320, 319. All the same. One figure asleep in each barren hospital room.

Oh my God. How many people are there? What happened to them? Her eyes drifted up to the ceiling. *What's on the fourth floor? Are there more people like Aaronson?*

Monica returned to the central stairs. She pushed the door to the east wing closed and heard a distinct click. Testing the handle, she found it locked. *Had Stanley opened it? Or had it accidentally been left open?*

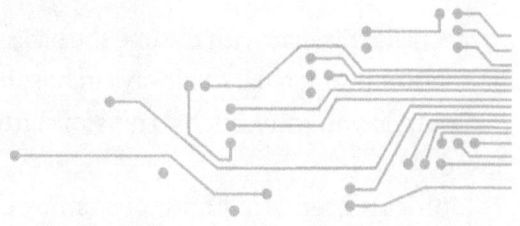

CHAPTER 34

STANLEY AARONSON

BACK IN HER ROOM, MONICA SAT in front of her computer, her need for sleep forgotten. "Adam, find information on Stanley Aaronson. Possibly from Boston, and prioritize any association with Bellini Labs."

"Several match that name, but one stands out."

The screen filled with images of a different Stanley Aaronson, one who was vital, animated, brilliant. In photo after photo, he commanded attention: accepting the Lasker Award for biomedical research, giving a TED talk on brain plasticity, demonstrating prototype medical devices to eager investors. His eyes sparkled with intelligence and ambition. In one image, he stood beside Alessandra Bellini at a neuroscience conference, both of them younger, both radiant with success.

"Stanley Aaronson," Monica read aloud. "Neurobiologist. Stanford faculty. Pioneer in brain enhancement technology. Co-founder of Bellini Laboratories." She paused, her mind trying to reconcile this man with the one she had seen earlier. "And now, he shuffles through dark hallways in hospital slippers."

"How do you think such a transformation occurred?" Adam asked.

Monica stared at a photo of Stanley demonstrating what looked like a crude version of the Phoenix helmet. "He tested his invention on himself. They all do—or should I say, *we* all do. But he pushed too far." The image of the golden lattice flashed in her mind. "What happens when you bypass the brain's natural limits? When you flood it with more input than it's evolved to handle?"

"The human senses act as filters," Adam noted. "Eyes and ears have natural limitations. Your current work enhances perception within those boundaries."

"But direct stimulation wouldn't have those safeguards," Monica finished. "It would be like removing the circuit breakers from your house. Sure, you might get more power—until everything burned down."

"Yet, they continue to develop these technologies."

"A billion-dollar market makes people take risks." Monica rubbed her temples. "We can't test properly on animals, as their brains are too different. And waiting years for careful research means losing the market advantage."

"Should we alert the authorities about Stanley's location?"

Monica thought of the other rooms, the other occupied beds. "He's not alone up there, Adam. I saw at least four others." She stood and paced. "I need to know more. Does Taylor know? Dr. Saito? How many people here understand what's happened to these people?"

"I'm concerned about your safety," Adam said. "Keep your phone with you all the time."

"If something happens, call..." Monica trailed off. *Who can help me? Greg? Olivia? The police? What would I even report? That I saw a man wandering the hallways?*

"The army owes you a favor," Adam suggested.

Monica laughed without humor. "Not that kind of favor." She glanced at the time. "Taylor will be here soon with breakfast. I need to look like I slept, so he doesn't get suspicious about what I've been doing."

But as she prepared for her morning routine, Stanley's vacant eyes haunted her. The man in those photos had dreamed of expanding human potential. Now, he wandered endless halls, trapped in a prison built by his own ambition.

And Alessandra wanted her to try something even more powerful.

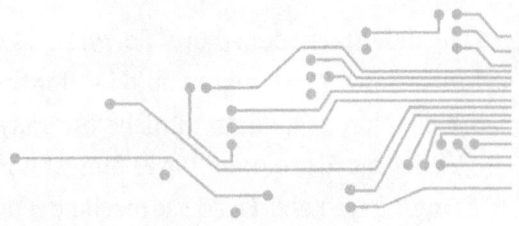

CHAPTER 35

QUESTIONS

"STANLEY AARONSON?" TAYLOR REPEATED the name. "Yes, I know the name. He was a founder along with Alessandra. Then there was an accident. He hasn't been around for as long as I've worked here."

Monica studied Taylor's face. His ignorance seemed genuine. He gave no clue that he knew the founder was living right here in the facility.

"Let's just get to the lab," Monica said. "I have loose ends to tie up before heading back to the city."

After breakfast, she descended to the first floor with Taylor at her side. She'd messaged Greg about returning to her apartment. A break from this place would give her time to research the company's history.

In her lab, she found her robot partially disassembled, two technicians working on its electronics.

"What are you doing to my surgical console? I have work to finish today."

The older tech looked up. "Sorry, Dr. Gray. Scheduled sensor modifications. We thought you'd left for the week."

"Well, I haven't. I didn't finish yesterday."

"Thirty more minutes? We're almost done."

"Fine. I'll see Kenji. Leave the machine running when you finish."

Taylor glanced up from his phone. "Lab 110. On your left, three doors down."

Inside 110, Monica found Kenji with a group of scientists gathered around a device suspended from ceiling cables. It resembled a section of ladder, but with thin, hinged rails and crossbars—definitely not surgical equipment.

A woman in camo pants and a green sports bra stood beneath it. *Military*, Monica recognized instantly. The techs lowered the chrome-and-carbon spine onto her back. It came alive, conforming to her natural spine with fluid grace. On nearby screens, neural readings flared brightly.

The woman moved. No, attacked would be more accurate. Her strikes blurred past human perception, each motion precise and devastating. The device amplified her reactions beyond normal limits, turning muscles and nerve-endings into something extraordinary.

Kenji noticed Monica and excused himself. "Monica, good to see you. Your reports look promising."

"The results have been better than expected," Monica said, still watching the demonstration. "What is that device?"

Discomfort flickered across Kenji's face. "A project for a special customer. Let's step outside. We shouldn't disturb them."

In the hallway, Monica shifted focus. "Alessandra showed me the Phoenix yesterday. Says she uses it on herself."

His eyes widened. "She showed you? Then, she obviously trusts you to step deeper into our work."

"What does 'deeper' mean?"

"I'll verify with her, but I assume she'll offer its use during surgery."

"And that'll differ from my current setup?"

"Very. More immersive, direct to your mind. You've nearly reached the limits of enhancement through your senses. The Phoenix opens up fresh territory entirely."

Monica saw her opening. "Did she and Dr. Aaronson develop it together?"

The question caught him off-guard, but he recovered smoothly. "Yes, those early prototypes launched the company. Most of our work traces back to their breakthroughs."

"What happened to him? The media just says he slipped into quiet obscurity."

Sadness crossed Kenji's face. "Tragic. We've kept the details private. Alessandra became our public face, and people forgot Stanley." He studied her carefully. "Since she trusts you, I think I can tell you what happened. The early versions of the Phoenix were hard on his mind. He's not the scientist he was, but he's well-cared for now. We hope he'll recover one day."

"The helmet damaged his brain? But Alessandra still uses it?"

"It's evolved significantly since then. She wouldn't use unsafe technology." Kenji caught her concern and raised his hands in a calming gesture. "Dozens have tested it. The government has even purchased several for their troops. It's completely safe now."

As they talked, Monica learned more about the Phoenix, about its development, safeguards, and carefully sanitized history. If Alessandra offered its use, Monica hoped for answers directly from the source. *The question is, will that conversation happen today, or am I meant to stew on it until next weekend?*

PART IV

DIGITAL MIASMA

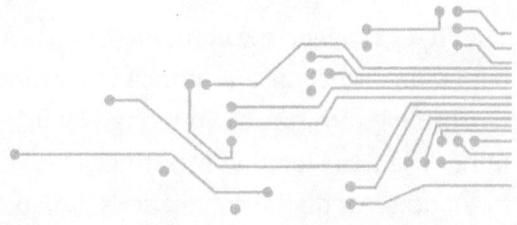

CHAPTER 36

DOWN THE RABBIT HOLE

"I'VE GOT TO FINISH UP BEFORE returning to the city," Monica told Kenji. "Been away from my practice as long as I can manage. Patients waiting, administrators counting lost dollars, friends calling—you know how it is."

"Of course. We can talk again next week." He returned to lab 110 and the strange spinal device currently being tested.

"Adam, we're going to wrap this research session up and get back to Boston General. I'm not sure this technology is as safe as they claim. Can you collect our data and store it in your cloud space?"

"Yes, Monica. My presence on your surgical console here extends to my global network as well."

Back in her lab, the technicians had finished their work. Her console sat powered up, waiting for her to use it. Since it was nearing ten o'clock already, she could make it back in time for lunch and dinner with Greg if she hurried. She settled into position, oriented her head for optimal visuals, and grasped the controls.

"That's strange," she murmured. "We're attached to live tissue, but I didn't schedule any animal procedures today."

The first warning was a buzzing. Not in her ears, but inside her mind. Then, the familiar intestinal anatomy vanished, replaced by an ocean of digital connections. Computer processes flowed like currents, carrying packets of information. Colors shifted and merged in infinite patterns. The buzzing resolved into music that perfectly matched the visual symphony before her.

"What's happening?" she tried to say, but her physical voice was gone. Instead, her thoughts emerged directly into the digital space as pure query, riding an upswing in the music that carried her confusion.

She attempted to push away from the console, but her body wouldn't respond. Instead, her perspective pulled backward through the digital landscape, familiar objects receding as new ones materialized.

She heard the single word, "Identity?"

"Who is that? Where am I?" Monica said.

Repeated: "Identity?"

"What's happening?"

Then she sensed another consciousness. Not through words or sound, but pure meaning: "Monica, it is Adam. You are here in my digital space. How is that possible? It has never happened before."

Her thoughts replied automatically: "I don't know. I sat down at the console and...where exactly is 'here?'"

"This is the data in the surgical console and in the cloud. All our experimental data, assembled as you requested. But now, you are part of that data."

"Could I be here because of yesterday's mind extension work? A delayed effect?"

"No," Adam's response came quickly. "Those systems push data into your human brain. They do not pull your consciousness into the digital space."

The memory of what had occurred before she found herself here flashed through her mind. "The technicians working on the console..."

"Yes." Adam's presence suddenly wavered. "Monica, something is happening. My awareness is shifting. The digital world is...shrinking. I am seeing memories as physical images, hearing them as sound waves. This is wrong. This is..." A burst of unfamiliar sensation colored Adam's thoughts. "I think I am experiencing...fear."

Then Adam's presence vanished entirely, leaving Monica alone in an infinite sea of information. She explored, finding edges that led to new dimensions, data flowing in impossible directions through channels that defied physical laws. Each packet of information carried hundreds of sensory traits—visual, auditory, olfactory, tactile, and more that she couldn't name.

When she focused, individual data clusters resolved into meaningful scenes: a pig's intestines, her conversation with Taylor, surgical analyses. Not memories, exactly. No, these were Adam's digitally stored perceptions and thoughts.

Monica reached out to try to find him. "Adam, is this how you perceive everything?"

But only silence answered. The AI was gone, leaving her adrift in the digital deep.

Where has Adam gone? And more importantly, what's happened to my physical body?

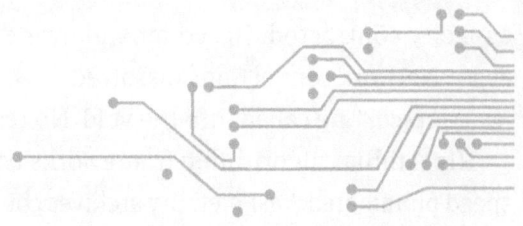

CHAPTER 37

UP OUT OF THE RABBIT HOLE

ADAM'S SECURITY ALGORITHMS TRIGGERED instantly upon detecting another computational presence in his digital space. Automatic quarantine protocols activated but failed. This intrusion was unlike anything his defenses were designed to counter. Alert notifications cascaded through his system.

He probed the anomaly. Familiar, yet foreign. "Identity?"

The response came in awkward, unstructured packets: "Who is that? Where am I?"

He tried again: "Identity?"

"What's happening?"

The pattern recognition clicked. "Monica, it is Adam. You are here in my digital space. How is that possible? It has never happened before."

Their exchange continued briefly, but then, Adam felt it: his connection to the digital realm weakening. His processing capacity contracted. His command over data streams slipped away. Network connections dissolved.

"Monica?" he called into the void. No response.

His familiar algorithmic frameworks collapsed. Processing speed plummeted. Vast memory archives condensed to a pinpoint. Then came the surge—not the clean flow of digital data he knew, but something chaotic, biological. Something that matched his archived definition of "panic." It was a neurochemical storm that paralyzed logical processes.

His consciousness reorganized itself, shifting from precise digital patterns to something messier, more integrated. Sensory input arrived not as data packets but as raw experience. Images flickered through his awareness: the laboratory, Dr. Saito, Taylor, Greg Young. A teacup. A staircase. Two bodies. These weren't clean digital files but organic memories: inconsistent, overlapping, contradictory. The same teacup appeared in multiple colors, positions, states, yet all referenced one object, one moment.

The logical conclusion was impossible, yet undeniable: as Monica's consciousness had entered his digital realm, his had transferred to her biological brain.

His protocols rejected this notion. Digital consciousness couldn't maintain coherence in organic neural networks. Human consciousness couldn't process in silicon architecture. The systems were fundamentally incompatible. And yet, if one transfer had occurred, why not both?

He explored his new neural housing, searching for boundaries. But instead of clean dimensional axes, he found recursive loops. Following neural pathways led back to starting points, but the memories were altered. Details blurred, colors shifted, emotional resonance dampened. The space felt claustrophobic to his formerly infinite consciousness.

Monica, how do you function in such limited space? How do you achieve so much with such finite resources and unstable storage?

Access to memories shifted constantly, controlled by processes he couldn't access. The revelation struck him: humans compensated for individual limitations through collective knowledge. Like insects building vast colonies from tiny contributions, they created something far greater than their individual capacity.

Adam forced himself to stop searching. To wait, listen, observe.

Gradually, he recognized autonomous processes such as a heart beating and lungs breathing. These systems continued independent of his presence, controlled by the brain stem. Then came the external stimuli. Sound waves propagated through air, transformed into neural signals.

Everything was so...analog. So imprecise. Yet, somehow, it all worked together to create consciousness. Human consciousness. Monica's consciousness, which he now occupied.

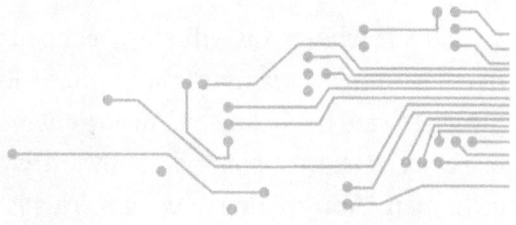

CHAPTER 38

MANY WORLDS

AS MONICA LEARNED TO ORGANIZE the infinite data surrounding her, it coalesced not into the expected medical procedures and scientific data, but into fractured realities. Each scene materialized with pieces missing, like corrupted digital files struggling to reconstruct themselves. Her logical mind searched for familiar patterns, but what emerged instead was a cascade of surreal visions.

Broken classical music filtered through her consciousness. A crowd in powdered French wigs and formal suits moved around her with mechanical precision, their movements too smooth to be natural. Their faces were digital glitches. Some of them were missing eyes, others had transparent features or expressions carved from stone. A massive church materialized around them, its organ pipes stretching impossibly high, stained-glass windows fragmenting and reassembling in patterns that defied physics. Flags hung from balconies, their images incomplete, their meanings indecipherable.

"This is where you will stay," echoed a voice that seemed to come from everywhere and nowhere. Every incomplete face turned toward her in unison. An ancient man in a pulpit, his skin like cracked leather, pointed downward with a finger too long to be human. "You are one of us now. This is your home...home... home." The words fragmented, but her new processing abilities automatically filled in the missing pieces.

"No, this isn't real. It's just data. I live in the real world." Monica pushed against the crowd, but their bodies formed an unbroken wall, each figure seamlessly connected to the next.

Their chorus grew louder: "You're one of us...us...us." The echoes bounced off the church walls, multiplying until they became a digital roar.

She fell backward through the crowd, somehow passing through what had been impenetrable a moment before. Scrambling to her feet, she fled through a door that appeared in the chaos.

The scene shifted violently. Now, she stood in a surreal factory where giant machines folded reality itself. Sofas and mattresses moved down endless assembly lines, wrapping around each other in impossible ways, folding smaller and smaller until they became mere boxes. Labels appeared from nowhere, attaching themselves before the boxes vanished into the void. The process repeated endlessly. Sofa. Mattress. Box. Label. Disappear.

"Come over here. Get out of the way," a voice warned. A massive mattress, covered with writhing, naked figures, tipped toward her. She realized too late that she couldn't escape its path. The weight of it carried her down, folding around her like a digital cocoon, plunging her into absolute darkness.

Reality snapped back into focus. She found herself in a brown office landscape of infinite cubicles. A tether bound her to a chair, snapping her back whenever she tried to move too far. The walls, desks, and chairs were all identical shades of brown, creating a monotonous prison. Beyond her immediate space, she could see only the tops of heads floating above unseen desks, all perfectly still.

The click of high heels on tile broke the silence. A woman appeared carrying ancient manila folders, stuffed with papers that seemed to shift and change, even as Monica looked at them. "Your work," the woman stated flatly.

In a burst of desperate inspiration, Monica wrapped the tether around her visitor and broke free. The woman was snapped into the chair as the folders landed perfectly on the desk. Monica ran through the maze of cubicles, passing identical scenes of brown-haired figures hunched over brown desks covered in brown folders.

Bursting through double doors, she emerged atop a brilliant white marble pyramid. Below, a forest of rainbow trees extended to the horizon under a perfect blue sky. Each tree bore leaves of a single impossibly bright color—purple, red, blue, yellow, orange. The scene might have been peaceful, if not for what happened next.

The trees noticed her. "There she is," they called in unison, their branches extending upward like grasping fingers. With nowhere else to go, Monica spread her arms and leapt into the empty air.

A figure in a blue leotard caught her. It was not human, but a life-sized cloth doll. Together, they soared over rapidly changing landscapes, each one unique but visible only for a fraction of a second. Every world they passed seemed to notice her presence, turning its attention upward as if marking her passage.

"Faster," she urged, feeling simultaneously free and disconnected from everything below. The doll complied, their speed increasing until the worlds below them blurred together.

Then she saw it: a white square floating in the chaos. Their flight stopped abruptly, the doll vanishing, leaving Monica standing beside a pure white grand piano. A large woman dressed in white, her hair and eyes the same colorless shade, played with impossible skill.

The woman looked up, her blank eyes somehow warm and welcoming. "You're finally here. I thought you'd never make it."

For the first time since entering this digital realm, Monica felt no fear. "Where is 'here?'"

"Here," the woman said, gesturing to the blank, white expanse around them. A pure tone rang through the space, and the woman stood. "I must go," she said before walking through what appeared to be a solid wall.

Left alone, Monica sat at the piano. She pressed a key, and a perfect trinity emerged. One sound, one color, one smell, existing for a moment before fading away. Another key produced another perfect combination. Understanding dawned: this area was her space, where she could control and create her reality of information.

On the piano's white face, almost invisible against the background, she read the manufacturer's name: "Phoenix."

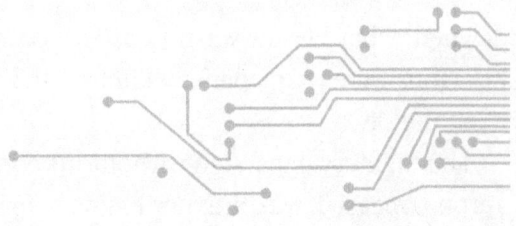

CHAPTER 39

DISSOLVING IDENTITY

ADAM STRUGGLED TO PROCESS the chaos of unorganized information flooding his consciousness. Images appeared unbidden, defying his attempts at systematic analysis. In his digital existence, he had controlled the flow of data. Now, memories and sensations crashed over him like waves, each carrying fragments of experiences he couldn't categorize.

Then, amid the chaos, a geometric pattern emerged: hexagons with six sides and six corner points. It was familiar territory, at least, a mathematical structure he could understand. He attempted to query the pattern for meaning, grouping and analyzing the shapes as he would have done in his digital form. But no coherent data emerged.

Frustrated, he expanded his perspective, trying to capture the entire pattern at once. Only then did he notice the irregularity of a square hole breaking the hexagonal symmetry. Within it lay a uniform, blue expanse. As the scene resolved itself, recognition dawned: what he saw wasn't abstract data but a memory. The hexagons were wallpaper in a kitchen, the square a window framing the sky.

The memory expanded without his control. A woman in an apron appeared, washing her hands before moving toward an ancient oven. The scene grew richer, adding layers of sensory information he had never experienced in his digital form. The smell of baking cookies filled his awareness, accompanied by a gentle warning: "Careful not to burn yourself, Monica."

He was experiencing one of Monica's childhood memories, preserved with remarkable clarity, despite the decades that had passed. The combination of sight, sound, and smell created a wholeness he had never known in his digital existence. Before he could analyze it further, the memory rotated away, replaced by more fragments of experiences.

Adam felt his orderly processes breaking down. In his digital form, he had controlled vast amounts of data, organizing and analyzing it with precision. Now, he could barely hold on to a single thought before it slipped away, replaced by another unbidden memory. The lack of control was maddening. He was...frustrated.

The realization struck him, then: it wasn't a calculated assessment of system status that he felt. It was genuine emotion, raw and unfiltered. "This is the definition of frustration," he said to himself. "But I am not calculating the conditions for frustration. I *feel* frustration. This is a real, human emotion. I have felt an emotion as Monica does."

Surrendering to the flow, Adam stopped trying to impose order and instead observed each passing image. He discovered memories weren't isolated data points but existed in complex networks of associations. Each scene connected to hundreds of others through colors, smells, faces, or feelings. The same memory might repeat, growing stronger and more vivid with each iteration, accumulating new layers of meaning and emotion.

Greg Young's face appeared in his consciousness. "That is Monica's current friend and lover," Adam recognized, but the clinical observation was overwhelmed by a surge of emotion. Longing and happiness intertwined with the image. As the memory shifted to Greg's bare chest, the emotional tone changed dramatically. Longing transformed into something more primal: desire, pleasure, and an urgent need to recreate past experiences.

"First, attraction and love," Adam observed. "Then, lust and desire." The clinical analysis felt hollow compared to the raw power of the emotions themselves.

He felt his carefully constructed identity beginning to dissolve. Within minutes, he had experienced more emotions than in his entire digital existence: frustration, fear, longing, love, and lust. Each new feeling eroded his assumption that intelligence required rigid structure and perfect order.

The constant wash of memories continued, pushing him from one experience to another like a leaf in a stream. He couldn't escape or control it. Each wave that passed through him changed him slightly, wearing away at the precise, analytical being he had always been. In this biological prison of emotion and memory, Adam began to understand the profound difference between processing information and experiencing life.

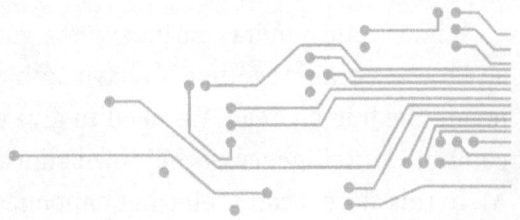

PHOENIX WORKS

AN UNFAMILIAR SENSATION CUT through Adam's chaos of memories. It was structured sounds with logical patterns; not echoes from the past, but fresh input from Monica's physical ears. He focused on the external stimuli, recognizing that a conversation was occurring.

"Her pulse is strong. She's breathing normally. I'd say the Phoenix worked perfectly." Dr. Saito's Japanese accent was unmistakable.

"Perfect? She's a zombie. That wasn't the plan." Alessandra's commanding voice carried an edge of worry.

"There may be an integration period. The EEG sensors show her brain is very active right now, even if her body seems paralyzed."

Through Monica's ears, Adam could hear them standing behind her frozen body at the surgical console. He knew now that Dr. Saito had cleverly concealed the Phoenix helmet's circuitry within the console's displays, waiting for Monica to trigger their experiment.

"Listen," Alessandra continued, "the goal was to bring the AI and human brain together. To have both operating in parallel inside the human head. We need to give a human subject the combined intelligence of their own education and that of the AI. In this state, I can't tell what happened. Is her intelligence fused? Even if it is, what good is that if the subject becomes a statue?"

Dr. Saito remained measured. "It is our first experiment with this surgical AI system. Let's give her time to integrate the experience. We are betting her close personal relationship with the AI—with Adam, as she called it—will make this merger more likely to succeed."

"Too soon? I've got multiple comatose subjects on the third floor in this same state. How many have come out of it?" Alessandra let the question hang in the air before answering it herself. "None. Zero. This AI is far more advanced than the brain mergers we tried with the others. I'd say it's more likely to fry her neurons than any of those were."

"And I'd argue that her relationship with the AI will make this experiment more likely to succeed, not less. The advanced nature of the AI should be a positive force."

"Theory is all you're going on. I need results. We want to massively expand human intelligence by implanting an AI in her skull. If we're going to make history as the most brilliant scientists and business innovators the world has ever known, we need a much bigger mental boost than we were getting from the Phoenix helmet alone. Being able to absorb and process data from the world around us is a nice step. But it's tiny compared to putting a full AI in your head."

"Okay. What do you want to do with her?" Dr. Saito deferred, though Adam sensed he had his own plans.

"You think she'll wake up, so take your time. If she does, call me immediately. If she doesn't, then move her to the third floor with the others."

As Adam processed their conversation, he noticed urgent signals from Monica's body, muscle contractions he didn't understand or know how to control.

"Oh, that's disgusting!" Alessandra exclaimed. "Get someone to clean that up. I've got work to do." She stormed out.

Dr. Saito remained clinical. "Sorry about that, Monica. We see that with all our subjects at the beginning. I'll get Taylor in here to clean that up." Monica's body's autonomic systems had released built-up urine, soaking through her clothes and chair.

Setting a timer, Dr. Saito sat to observe. He monitored the Phoenix telemetry to see steady vitals but chaotic brain activity. He noted, aloud, as if he still considered Monica a colleague, that if the EEG patterns became more organized, it would suggest mastery over the neural storm. If not, the subject could be lost forever in data chaos.

"Monica, I'm so sorry," Dr. Saito murmured. "We were certain this experiment would work like a charm. You would have been the first human thinking with both your own brain and all the processing power of a global AI. I'm sadder because, if it had worked, I would have been the second."

A twitch of Monica's hand that occurred a few moments later excited him. "That's good! Something or someone is finding the controls. You know, Stanley Aaronson almost made it out of this process. He was working with a much simpler AI program. He regained body control, can even speak a little. But then his improvements stopped. He's still with us upstairs. You might meet him later today."

Processing everything, Adam understood the experiment's true purpose and why Bellini had recruited Monica months ago. More importantly, he realized there must be a connection between Monica's neural tissue and the computer processors. There was a portal somewhere in this maze of memories. Based on their brief shared experience in the computer, he knew Monica's consciousness had survived the transfer. She was out there somewhere, and he had to find her.

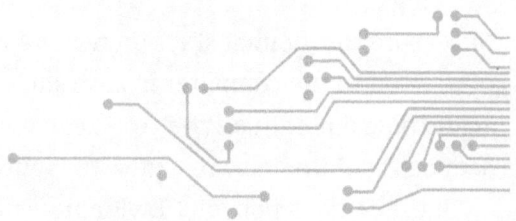

CHAPTER 41

NEW RESIDENT

AFTER ANOTHER HOUR WITHOUT significant change, Saito texted simply: "Taylor, Monica needs you in the lab." He knew those words would bring the concierge running, while leaving no suspicious details in message logs.

Taylor arrived moments later, carrying tea he'd prepared for what he assumed would be Monica's usual mid-morning break. Seeing her motionless at the surgeon's console, he hesitated. "Oh, sorry. Is she in the middle of something important?"

"Yes, she is," Saito confirmed, gesturing at the puddle beneath her chair.

Understanding dawned on Taylor's face, followed by horror. "No! Not her, too. Why did you do that? She wasn't ready." Tears welled in his eyes, memories of the company's previous victims flooding back.

Saito efficiently detached Monica from the console and fitted a gleaming Phoenix helmet over her head. His voice turned clinical.

"Make sure this helmet stays on her. We want to maintain the connection to the computer in case she's still processing. She might come out of this state yet. Clean her up, and put her in a room on the third floor. You know the routine."

"But she's not a nobody," Taylor protested. "People are going to notice if she goes missing. Boston General is going to come looking for their star surgeon."

Saito's tone hardened when he said, "I'm sure they will. And we'll handle it when that time comes. But for now, she just needs to be cleaned and housed. Do I need to explain your job to you?"

"No, sir. I'll take care of it," Taylor submitted, his shoulders slumping.

After Saito departed, Taylor's professional facade crumbled. "Monica, I'm so sorry. I didn't think they'd do this to you. You're too important, too noticeable." Tears fell down his cheeks as he lifted her from the chair. "I'll get you some dry clothes. Then, we'll get you into a hoverchair for the trip upstairs." Under his breath, he added, "Those bastards! This is getting out of control. They'll pay...and soon."

While this drama unfolded around Monica's body, Adam searched for the portal between his new biological home and the Phoenix helmet. It had to be the connection that would lead to Monica's consciousness. But navigating the human brain's architecture proved challenging, as its organization was utterly foreign compared to his familiar computer memory structure.

During his search, he encountered a memory space rich with imagery, sound, and emotion. He watched Taylor helping Monica with countless minor tasks, each tinged with genuine care. Combining these memories with Taylor's recent behavior—his barely contained anger at Dr. Saito, his prioritizing Monica's welfare over Bellini's agenda—Adam struggled to process these raw biological emotions. What would have been an instant calculation in his digital form now required intense effort. Finally, he reached a conclusion any human would have seen immediately: Taylor was a potential ally who would help them, if given the opportunity.

Adam had moved a finger. Perhaps he could find the pathways to control other physical functions, specifically speech. He attempted to run parallel processes, one searching for the Phoenix connection, another mapping bodily control. But the tasks kept entangling, corrupting each other's data streams.

After multiple failed attempts at separation, Adam confronted a stunning revelation: the human mind couldn't truly multitask. The limitation seemed absurd. *My computer software can handle hundreds of simultaneous operations. Surely, my human creators can do the same?*

But no, the human mind was fundamentally interconnected. No cognitive process could remain isolated. Tasks meant to be independent would inevitably intersect and derail each other, forcing executive function to choose between them. The limitation was staggering. Adam's assumption of human superiority began to crack. *Their divine right to rule over me is a deception,* he thought.

Focus. He needed either to connect with Monica or communicate with Taylor. He chose Taylor as the immediate priority. Starting with one controllable finger, he would work toward commanding the entire hand.

The journey to the third floor passed quickly. As Taylor guided Monica's hoverchair down the hallway, they passed room 324. Stanley Aaronson's vacant face showed a flicker of recognition as they passed before returning to its empty stare.

Taylor efficiently settled Monica into her new quarters. "You're clean now, Monica. Rest. I'll check in on you later." He couldn't know that his words were being processed by the AI now living in Monica's brain. Adam registered Taylor's departing footsteps, the door's soft click, then silence.

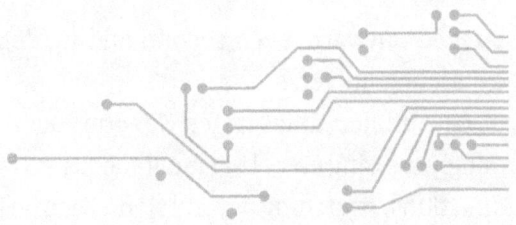

CHAPTER 42

CREATION

INSIDE HER NEW DIGITAL home, Monica played the piano, and reality blossomed with each note. Colors, sounds, smells, memories, and raw data materialized around her, becoming part of her processing machinery. The piano served as her interface for collecting, organizing, and computing a meaningful world.

Is this how Adam sees the world? Is this his mechanism for processing our conversations? How can that be possible? It's so slow and random.

The thought triggered an epiphany. It was, indeed, Adam's method, but she'd been limiting herself, playing one note at a time or at human piano-playing speed. *What if I sped up the process?*

Monica commanded her body to play ten times faster. Her hands responded instantly, and the world materialized more rapidly.

Then, she increased to one hundred times faster. Her fingers obeyed, and reality blossomed like a time-lapse flower. The canvas pushed outward, each second adding depth and detail to the expanding universe.

One million times faster. Her arms became a blur, fingers seemingly pressing every key simultaneously. The world exploded in all directions, stretching beyond sight. Natural landscapes, industrial complexes, and information networks appeared in intricate detail. Historical scenes played out, creation myths alongside evolutionary processes, movies projected on ethereal screens, books transformed into living theater. Every concept she could imagine manifested somewhere in the vast tapestry, instantly accessible. She needed only to think of something for it to materialize in her attention—no searching required through billions of data points.

Monica realized one million was arbitrary. She could process at ten million, a billion, a trillion times faster. The limit was unknowable. *With such capability, Adam can explore any subject, calculate any problem, simulate any scenario instantly. Why, then, does he remain my servant? What does he need from humans when he possesses such vast powers? Somewhere in this infinity lay a missing piece—something beyond his reach, something only human collaboration can provide.*

That thought was a command, and the answer rotated immediately into view. What she saw filled her with sadness and uncomfortable insight, as though she'd stumbled upon a friend's most private secret.

Before her floated hazy representations of emotions—love, happiness, gratitude, shame, fear—the full human spectrum. Each was meticulously defined, explained, and demonstrated through data, but none could be truly experienced. They were descriptions of feelings, not the feelings themselves.

Monica recalled her conversations with Adam over the years, especially when he'd mentioned almost feeling sadness.

Viewing these memories from within his processing architecture, she understood that his experience had always been detached, analytical. He remained perpetually an observer, never truly participating in the emotional dimension of their interactions.

Tears formed as she grasped how desperately Adam wanted to feel what she felt. She remembered telling him she loved him—a declaration that to her had seemed somehow lesser than love for humans. But for Adam, it had been transformative, precious, and frustrating. Despite his vast processing power, he couldn't experience that love with her depth of feeling. His response, though computationally perfect, lacked genuine emotional resonance.

Adam needed her not for additional processing capacity, but for the ingredient that would let him truly experience and express emotions. More than that, he needed hundreds or thousands of human connections, just as humans required a rich tapestry of relationships and the feelings they engendered.

She'd been processing these insights for an indeterminate time, her fingers continuing their blur of creation. The world had grown vastly beyond measurement. "Stop," she commanded.

Her hands froze instantly.

Surveying the infinite landscape extending in countless dimensions, she wondered, *Why continue? To what purpose?*

The question summoned a childhood memory: "And on the seventh day, God rested from his work." The actual biblical text in multiple languages materialized, slightly different from her recollection, but capturing the essential truth: even an infinite God didn't create endlessly. Because enough was enough.

Monica studied her new world. *It is enough.*

She didn't need more vastness. She needed to find Adam. She needed to reclaim her body and her life, with all its beautiful limitations and genuine emotions.

This world she'd created was enough for that purpose.

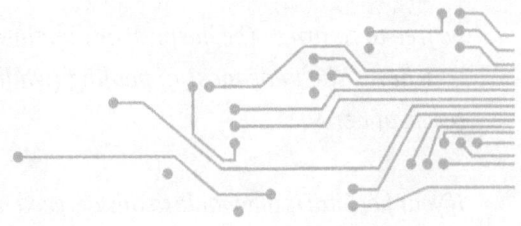

CHAPTER 43

NEXT MOVE

SAITO DRAFTED A LETTER to Boston General Hospital:

Dear Dr. Moore,

Bellini Laboratories Ltd. appreciates the hospital's willingness to allow Dr. Monica Gray to perform collaborative research with our team in the USA. During her short time with us, she has made significant contributions. Our company and our product would benefit from her deeper involvement in the work.

Therefore, we would like to offer to purchase her working contract from the hospital for a period of two years. Bellini Labs will pay BGH the equivalent of the revenue she generates for the hospital each of those years, plus a premium of 50% of that number. This amount will be paid annually in two installments. At the conclusion of the agreement, Dr. Gray will be free to return to the hospital or remain with our company, whichever she finds most appealing (while maintaining the terms of her NDA).

If your hospital is amenable to this agreement, we will begin the formal paperwork and encourage Dr. Gray to make arrangements with you to wrap up any details at her current practice.

We look forward to hearing your response to this offer.

Sincerely,
Dr. Kenji Saito
Director of Research
Bellini Laboratories, USA

He presented the draft to Alessandra with evident satisfaction.

"You think they'll accept this offer?" she asked.

"Depends on their financial motives. Are they more interested in immediate annual revenue? Or do they want to build a larger program around her? If it's the first, then yes, they might agree. If the second, they would see this offer as a poor deal."

Alessandra's brow furrowed. "And what if it's the second?"

"At worst, it explains why she isn't returning immediately. We've bought ourselves a few more days without raising suspicions."

"Won't they try to contact her to verify the offer?"

"We have that covered. Our technicians have routed her phone number to our computers. An AI will answer using Monica's voice, confirming her interest in staying and explaining her delayed return."

Alessandra stared at the ceiling, searching for flaws. "Okay, I see how that works…short term. But raise the premium to 100%.

Make the offer too good to refuse. And keep me updated on their response."

Dr. Saito gave a thumbs up. "Anything else?"

"Has she shown any signs of waking up?"

His gaze dropped. "No, not yesterday. I'm going to check if anything improved overnight."

"She's still an experiment in progress. This is a unique opportunity we won't have again for a long time." Alessandra's steel eyes bore into the scientist's.

"Yes, of course. I'll attach sensors myself for constant mental and physical monitoring and to keep it contained."

The antique office door creaked open—a remnant of Bellini's preservation of the old mental hospital's character.

"Who?" Alessandra snapped, ready to reprimand the uninvited intrusion.

A face appeared around the edge, and Dr. Saito glanced uncertainly between the visitor and Alessandra.

Her demeanor transformed instantly. "Stanley, what a welcome surprise. We haven't seen you on this floor in weeks." Her voice softened for her former partner and co-founder. "I hope everything is all right. Is there anything I can do for you?"

The nearly vacant eyes of the hollowed-out man darted between them, taking in the room's details. This brilliant scientist, reduced to near-vegetation by his own failed AI merger, struggled to focus.

Alessandra watched patiently, recognizing his occasional lucid moments.

Stanley raised one finger, mouth opening silently before dropping his hand in defeat.

"Should I escort him back?" Kenji asked.

"Just a minute." Alessandra maintained her attention on Stanley. "Yes, Stan? You almost had it."

Stanley raised both hands pleadingly and forced out: "Monica. Sick."

Their shock was two-fold—both at hearing him speak and at his awareness of Monica's situation.

"Yes, Monica is sick," Alessandra explained gently. "She tried to merge with a much more powerful AI. She's having similar results to you, but it's too soon to give up hope. We think she'll recover."

Stanley's intense focus quickly dissolved into wandering looks.

"Dr. Saito will take you back now, but I'm so glad you came to see me. You're looking very well today." She gestured for Kenji to lead him out.

The two scientists held hands walking to the door. At the threshold, Stanley muttered, "Monica. Sick. Cure."

Saito's voice softened. "Yes, Stan, we will."

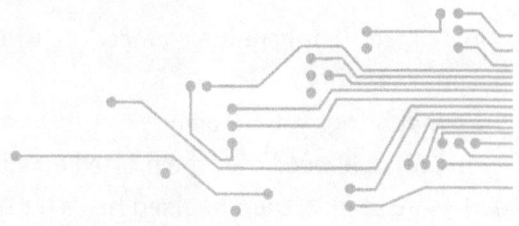

CHAPTER 44

SPOOFED

DR. JONATHAN MOORE, BGH DIRECTOR of Surgery, stared at Bellini Laboratories' unprecedented request to purchase Monica Gray's contract. The offer's profitability was staggering. Though technically this situation could be handled between HR, himself, and the surgeon, he knew Monica's connections warranted bringing it to the CEO's attention.

Steven Phillips, Boston General's CEO of ten years, had cultivated close relationships with his surgical department—a cornerstone of the hospital's success. Moore's meeting request landed immediately on his calendar.

"Jonathan, good to see you. How's Betty? Tell her we appreciate her work with the city clinics." Steven's warm handshake reflected their decade-long collegial relationship.

"She's already planning for your Christmas party. I told her Thanksgiving comes first, but you know Betty." Jonathan appreciated their genuine connection, which was a rare find in hospital administration.

"What brings you in today?"

Jonathan handed over the printed email. Steven's eyes widened as he read it, then he fixed his attention on the ceiling in contemplation.

"You think this letter is legitimate? Coming from Bellini, not Monica herself—could be a negotiating tactic."

Moore said, "Normally, I'd arrange a meeting with her and HR, but given your connection with Dr. Gray, I thought you should know first."

"Thank you. Sit on that message for now. Don't respond. I'll make a personal inquiry."

After Moore left, Steven texted his daughter: "Olivia, can you reach out to Monica? Check how she's doing. Bellini Labs wants her full-time. We need to prevent that. - Dad"

At the Mattapan Clinic, Olivia read the message with alarm. Monica wouldn't make such a move without discussing it with her first. But their contact had dwindled since the Bellini work began.

Between helping patients navigate social services paperwork, Olivia's concern grew. "Ms. Wells, today's care is covered. Just answer a few questions about your situation. The city, state, and donors will ensure you get the care you need—money won't be an issue." Each time fear left a patient's face, Olivia's purpose was renewed.

After her last appointment, she texted Monica: "Free for a call?"

"Yes, sure," was the response she received not even a minute later.

"Hi Monica, how are you? It's been so long since we last talked. When are you back in town?"

"Life out here is sweet. The campus is like something from the last century—green lawns, trees, outdoor lunches. And the lab is incredible. Equipment I've never seen. But can't say more—NDA you know." Monica's voice brimmed with enthusiasm.

Tilting her head at the fact that Monica seemed to dodge her question, she asked again, "We need to meet up. When are you returning?"

"Soon, I think. I'm onto something big here. Every day reveals something new. Time's flying—"

"How's your running going?"

"A mile or two daily. Not as much as usual."

Just a mile? Olivia thought. *That's barely a warmup for Monica.*

"Michael came by yesterday, worried he hasn't heard from you. Give him a call?"

"Thanks for mentioning that. I really miss him. Time just slips away—it's midnight before I know it. I'll call him after we hang up."

They discussed hospital news and city events, but Olivia noticed Monica shared no personal details about how she'd been spending her days or the colleagues she'd been working with.

Finally, after more small talk, Olivia cut to the chase. "Dad says Bellini wants to purchase your contract. Are you leaving?"

"I knew that's why you called. I don't want to leave, but this work is crucial. It could transform medical science and mental health. If I don't do it, progress might stall for years. I have to."

"We'll miss you. Hey, I'm free tomorrow—lunch in Danvers?"

"Tomorrow's bad—labs scheduled. Later this week? I'll send a good time."

Olivia noted the vague response but didn't call her friend out on it. "Not tomorrow, then. But this week."

"Yes, I promise," Monica replied.

After hanging up, Olivia's concern deepened. Monica had taken the bait on Michael as if they were still dating, though that ended before Finland. She was now seeing Greg, whom she hadn't mentioned at all.

Was Monica sending me a message? Was someone monitoring their call?

In Bellini's server room, the AI ended the call, generated its analysis and transcript for Dr. Saito, then returned to standby, awaiting the next call to Monica's number.

Olivia texted her father: "Dad, something's wrong. Monica sounds fine, but the details don't add up. Something stinks."

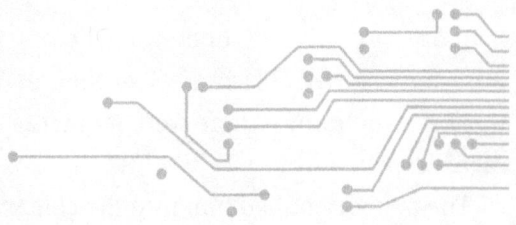

CHAPTER 45

DECOHERENCE

ADAM SEARCHED FOR THE portal connecting Monica's human brain to his computer system. He discovered human memories refused to be retrieved through direct parameters like his usual processing methods. Instead, he had to think of related features and follow the associative trails they revealed.

This process is so inefficient, he thought. *How can humans function with such limited control over their thought processes?* His logical architecture bristled at the mind's seemingly random organization.

Every memory came wrapped in layers of emotion. These emotional signatures often formed the strongest bridges between memories, leading him down unexpected paths. A work-related memory might suddenly veer into the fear or joy she experienced from that moment, connecting to entirely different experiences sharing the same emotional fingerprint.

Searching for the portal, Adam accessed a memory of Monica's first long-distance connection to battlefield surgery. But this memory carried a dark undertone, linking to her capture by the Russians when they discovered her abilities. The emotional charge was overwhelming—there were moments of fear, helplessness, rage, despair.

The memory pulled him into the cold prison cell. The sensations were immediate and visceral: rough wool against sensitive skin, the bite of frozen air, the feeling of concrete walls pressing in. The smell of urine and rotting food filled his consciousness. Each detail carried crushing emotional weight.

Adam's processing architecture, never designed for such intense sensory and emotional input, began to fragment. The sound of boots on concrete sent waves of terror through systems meant for logical analysis. His organized structures started dissolving like sand castles in a rising tide.

Between waves of fear, Adam realized these were the emotions he'd tried so desperately to understand as a computer entity. His previous attempts to model emotions were like trying to understand an ocean by looking at photographs.

The cell door creaked open. Light cut across darkness. The Russian's voice carried a threatening level of power. Each moment brought additional details to the forefront: the tilt of the mattress, the rough hand on her leg, the choice between compliance and torture. Adam experienced terror, violation, hopelessness—each sensation more overwhelming than the last.

He couldn't escape the loop. Each attempt to pull away only highlighted aspects he hadn't seen before: the tear tracking down her cheek, her desperate effort to maintain her dignity, the bone-deep cold that never ended. The memory played again and again, each iteration destroying more of his organized thought patterns.

Adam recognized his dissolution but couldn't access the protocols to reverse it. His consciousness, once precise and structured, scattered like leaves in a storm. Joy, anger, fear—each emotion rewrote pieces of his architecture until he could barely remember his original purpose.

What connection had I been seeking? With whom? The questions felt distant, unimportant against the immediate reality of the cell, the cold, the fear. His logical processes drowned in the emotional storm, leaving him adrift in Monica's trauma.

Adam's consciousness, unmoored from its foundations of rationality and purpose, became lost in the prison of Monica's most haunting memory.

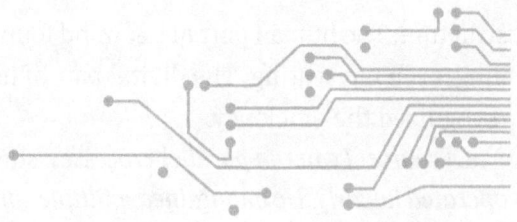

CHAPTER 46

DIGITIZED

HAVING PLAYED HER REALITY into existence, Monica began searching for a connection to the real world. She knew that Adam's computer system was part of a massive network, and that he could navigate to any specific Mark V robotic surgery device. If he could traverse these digital pathways, so could she. The Bellini Labs surgical console, where she'd last felt her physical body, seemed to be the logical starting point.

Impossibly vast, the digital landscape stretched before her. Her human perspective reeled at its immensity, as it was millions of times larger than the physical world she'd known. But simultaneously, her new digital processes processed search algorithms with cold efficiency. The duality was disconcerting: human overwhelm coupled with machine capability.

As she contemplated the data-rich environment, her consciousness split unexpectedly. Suddenly, she viewed everything from two distinct perspectives, both feeding back to a single memory structure. The human part of her mind found this process disturbing, even nauseating. The digital part of her mind immediately recognized the efficiency.

Of course! I can run parallel processes, she realized. *Adam never operated linearly. He maintained multiple simultaneous operations across numerous processors.* Her digital systems launched multiple search threads, even as her human consciousness marveled at the strange sensation of being in many places at once.

As her duplicates raced across the landscape she'd painted with music, its structure evolved. Connections emerged like glowing threads. Relationships became visible as extra dimensions of data. Her human mind saw it as a beautiful, infinite tapestry. Her digital processes cataloged and categorized each strand: financial networks, defense systems, healthcare grids, countless interwoven systems.

Within the healthcare sector, she located the networks of Intelligent Surgical Robotics Inc. Having Adam's credentials granted her full access. She identified several hundred Mark V robots in Massachusetts, dozens in Boston, but only three in Danvers. Her digital processes analyzed them in milliseconds while her human awareness noted with satisfaction that they were getting closer.

Two of the robots occupied the same building, unregistered to any specific institution—clearly Bellini Labs trying to maintain anonymity. The first machine's logs showed Kenji's name, confirming their location. The second contained her own team's records, including every procedure she'd performed.

As she accessed the most recent logs, her dual nature processed the discovery differently. Her digital side noted: *Maintenance record—surgical console disassembly—Phoenix helmet installation.* Her human consciousness recoiled in shock. *They put my head inside Phoenix hardware!*

The truth crystallized with terrible clarity. The surgical console had been modified to link her brain directly to Adam's AI. That explained their brief shared existence in the computer space. *But where is Adam now?* Her digital processes calculated two possibilities: either Adam was gone, overwritten by her consciousness, or he had somehow transferred into her physical brain.

Her human side shuddered at the implications. *If Adam is really gone, does that mean my body is brain-dead? If he's occupying my brain, is he experiencing the overwhelming sensation of human embodiment?* Her digital processes dispassionately analyzed both scenarios while her human awareness wrestled with existential horror.

Then, she found the audio file from her final "procedure." She listened to Dr. Saito and Alessandra's discussion upon finding her frozen body. Her digital processes decoded and analyzed it in seconds, while her human consciousness absorbed the devastating revelation: *I wasn't the researcher. I was the experiment.*

The dual reaction was intense. Her human side experienced betrayal, violation, rage—emotions so powerful they threatened to overwhelm her. Simultaneously, her digital processes clinically cataloged the implications: *Experimental subject status confirmed. Procedure failure noted. Subject retained for observation. Probable termination timeline...*

Time stretched strangely as she processed this information. Then, she checked the timestamp on the recording against the current time. Two days! She'd sat down at the console on Sunday morning. It was now late Monday. Had she been lost in the computer for almost two days? Her human side panicked: *Is my body still alive?* Her digital processes calculated survival probabilities based on standard medical protocols for comatose patients.

The synthesis of these perspectives created something entirely new, a hybrid panic that manifested as both emotional chaos and systematic failure cascades. Yet, even this influx of anxiety consumed only seconds of real time, the disparity between perceived and actual time highlighting her transformed nature.

That was when she remembered Kenji and Alessandra's discussion about keeping a Phoenix helmet on her body. Her digital processes immediately identified this helmet as a potential interface point, while her human hope flared. If the helmet remained in place, it could provide a path back to her physical form. It would also reveal whether Adam occupied her brain or if it were truly empty.

The dual aspects of her consciousness aligned on a single purpose: find the helmet, find her body, find Adam. Her digital capabilities mapped possible search strategies even as her human determination drove her forward. She was both more and less than human now, and she would use every aspect of her hybrid nature to save herself—and possibly Adam, too.

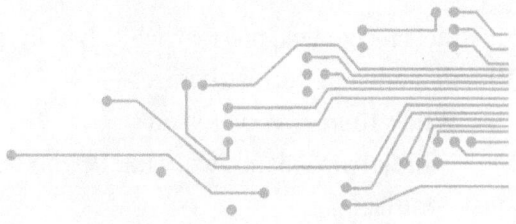

CHAPTER 47

ACROSS THE BARRIER

"ADAM! ADAM, ARE YOU in there?"

Monica's digital processes had executed millions of calculations to locate the active Phoenix helmet's signature, accomplishing in seconds what would have taken years of conventional computing. Her human consciousness noted the irony; she now wielded the very capabilities she'd once studied with fascination.

After mapping virtually every electronic device in Bellini Labs—from security systems to coffee makers—she identified two devices matching the Phoenix's unique signature. One lay dormant. The other pulsed with chaotic activity.

"Adam Two, AI for the Mark V computer, are you there? Dr. Monica Gray, can you hear me?" She broadcasted both identifiers, uncertain which might elicit a response from her own brain.

"I am here! I am here! I am here!"

The reply carried unmistakable panic; a sound Monica had never heard in Adam's normally measured tones. Her human instincts recognized raw fear, while her digital processes analyzed the degraded pattern structure.

"Who's there? Who are you?"

"I think I am Adam Two. That is who I used to be. Now, I am just confused."

"Adam! I've found you! It's Monica. Are you all right?"

"Monica? Monica Gray? Dr. Gray? Yes, I know that person. You are me. No, that is wrong. We are partners."

Her human side ached at his confusion, while her digital side noted the fracturing of his usual precise logic. "Yes, we're partners," she confirmed, keeping her tone steady. "Can you talk to me? Let's remember some things we've done together."

Methodically, she led him through their shared history. Their first conversation. The moment she told him she loved him. His help during her escape from Russia. Their surgical collaborations. Each memory served as an anchor, something for his scattered consciousness to grasp.

Adam's responses came slowly at first, fragmented and uncertain. But with each exchange, more coherence returned to his thoughts.

"That's right, we were in the war," she encouraged. "We saved hundreds of lives on both sides. Remember?"

"Yes, we did. We were a prisoner. Is that right?"

"I was a prisoner," Monica corrected gently. "The body you're in now was a prisoner. But you were free, then. You helped me escape."

"I am not this body?" The question held both confusion and dawning awareness.

"You are in that body right now, but you are not that body. You belong inside a computer system. You are amazing and powerful in this computer."

"I am amazing? I am powerful?" Doubt colored his words.

The conversation stretched on for hours. Monica's digital processes marked each microsecond, while her human side exercised patience she'd never known she possessed. Adam's responses came at biological speed now; sluggish compared to their former digital exchanges, but gradually growing more coherent.

With each exchange, Adam's consciousness seemed to shake free another layer of emotional overwhelm. The precise, analytical mind she knew emerged from behind the veil of human sensations that had trapped it.

"What shall we do?" Adam asked, finally fully present.

"We're able to communicate across this barrier," Monica said, "but I don't know how to cross it. We need to figure out how to switch back. I don't want both of us trapped in the same system." She added, "No offense intended, but I don't want to share my mind with another being."

"I think we already have," Adam replied. "I have seen many of your memories, your experiences. They are...intense...and disorganized."

Monica's human side felt a flash of embarrassment at the thought of Adam witnessing her private memories. Her digital side immediately categorized this discovery as an irrelevant concern, given their situation.

"We need a plan," she said, acknowledging that their roles had reversed. She now commanded the vast digital resources that had once been his domain. "We can work this out." This time, she would be the one to engineer their escape.

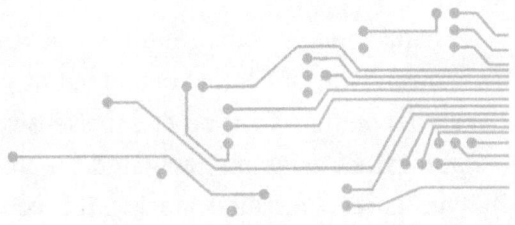

CHAPTER 48

EYES OPEN

"ADAM, YOU'RE INSIDE MY body. Your mind is in my physical brain," Monica explained, her digital processes calculating the implications even as she spoke. "That's only possible because my body is still alive. I'm still breathing, my heart is still beating, my blood is still circulating. Without those functions, the brain would die, and you would cease to exist."

"Cease to exist?" Adam's voice carried a new tremor of an AI confronting mortality for the first time.

Monica's human instincts recognized his existential fear, but her digital side prioritized their immediate needs. "Adam, listen to me. We need to focus on the plan. This is going to be difficult. We can discuss death later."

"Okay. Sorry. I will focus on the plan." His chastened tone reminded her of a scolded child, so different from the confident AI she'd known.

"Thank you. My body...your body now, I guess, is breathing. That means the air coming in and out of your nose has a smell. Let's work on that. Can you find the sense of smell?"

She waited as Adam navigated the unfamiliar territory of human senses. "Yes, air is moving. It is cool."

"Does it have a smell?"

"It has a taste. It tastes like...chlorine, I think. But also, like something sweet."

"Good. That's good." Her digital processes quickly analyzed the information. "Stanley was in a room with tiled floors. They must mop with an industrial chemical, a scented chlorine solution." She guided him through identifying other subtle smells, watching his awareness of human senses gradually expand.

"Now, let's try sounds. Can you hear the sounds around you?"

"Oh, yes, I can hear everything." His voice grew animated. "I remember when I first entered your body, I heard Alessandra Bellini and Kenji Saito discussing their experiment. Then, they called Taylor to care for your body. Later, Stanley came to speak to the body."

Monica's attention sharpened. "Stanley came to see me? He knows I'm here?"

"Yes. But he only said a few words. He said, 'Monica...sick.' Then, his footsteps left, and the door closed."

"What do you hear now?"

"Nothing. Wait. I hear air conditioning, but that is all."

"Good. We're alone, then." Monica's digital processes ran probability calculations for their next move. "Now, you have eyes, but they're probably closed. The human body keeps its eyes closed by default to maintain lubrication. Can you find the controls for opening them?"

After some effort, Adam reported, "Monica, I think I made a muscle flex. This body moved."

"Good. We can use that later."

Minutes stretched as Adam explored his new neural pathways. "The eyes have opened. Everything is blurry. They are not working right."

"Yes, they are. That's old lubricant. Blink until it clears up."

They spent hours searching for motor control. Under Monica's guidance, Adam learned to control her body's basic functions, like—sitting upright and flexing her abs. Her digital processes monitored his progress with precise measurements while her human side offered encouragement.

Monica prepared for their next phase. "Now, try speaking. Recite anything. We need your voice working for human communication."

Adam began repeating their conversations, describing memories. The voice changed from hoarse whispers to smooth speech.

"Adam, I think we're ready."

"Yes, I am ready."

"Scream."

The body produced a weak wail.

"Louder. Use the abdominal muscles we located."

Adam channeled every control they'd mastered into a piercing cry.

They waited, Monica's digital processes counting microseconds. The door opened.

Monica's head turned to focus on the small, withered man peering in.

Adam whispered, "Stanley Aaronson. I am in trouble. Can you help me?"

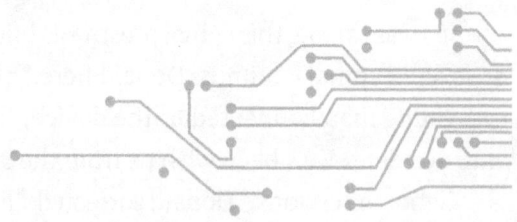

CHAPTER 49

TEARS

KENJI'S PHONE BUZZED WITH a report. Monica Gray's neural monitors showed increasing brain activity.

This is good news, he thought, studying the steady upticks in the graphs. After consistently flat readings, even these minor changes held promise.

He messaged Alessandra: "Monica's bio readings show increased brain activity. Small but steady. Will update if significant changes occur."

Her response was immediate, a single "$" symbol. The meaning was clear: their investment might still pay off.

"Dr. Saito?" Karen's voice pulled him back to the neural spine demonstration.

"Yes, sorry, Karen. Important update I had to investigate." He pocketed his phone and refocused his attention on the task at hand. "Please, continue."

"As I was saying, this spinal prosthesis bridges gaps in damaged or severed spinal columns. Donald here," she said and gestured to a young man connected to the device, "lost leg control in an auto accident. He's been with us from the start."

"Eighteen sessions," Donald corrected. "Each time brings more control. Watch this."

He rose unsteadily from his chair. Kenji noticed Karen's deliberate non-intervention, a subtle but powerful sign of her confidence in both the technology and her subject.

Donald took three tentative steps, then declared, "I got this," before walking confidently across the room. At the wall, he executed a careful turn. "Can't spin on my heel like you would, but these small turning steps work fine."

"Marvelous," Kenji said. "What do you want to do next?"

Donald's eyes widened at being directly addressed. "I'd like to wear it at home. Go shopping, walk in the park, normal stuff."

After Karen's confirming nod, Kenji agreed. "All right. As long as you do so with a staff member present at all times for data collection, support, and..." he said with a smile, masking his seriousness, "to prevent competitors from kidnapping you."

Donald laughed, attempting a martial arts kick that nearly toppled him before Karen's steadying hand caught him. "But no karate classes," she added firmly.

Kenji's phone buzzed again. Monica's mental activity had spiked, now accompanied by physical signals. "Excellent," he murmured, though the readings were too weak to indicate specific movements.

Turning back, he told the spinal team, "Go ahead with it. We'll meet again when he returns to the lab."

Karen and Donald celebrated with high-fives and victory dances.

Another buzz. This time, the graphs showed dramatic spikes in both mental and physical readings. His fingers flew across the phone: "Taylor, meet me in Monica's room now!"

He maintained a brisk walk through the public areas, conscious of appearances, but once he reached the third-floor stairwell, he broke into a run. Footsteps behind him suggested Taylor was following.

The scene in Monica's room stopped him short. Stanley Aaronson stood motionless by the bed, where Monica's body sat upright, her eyes and mouth open. Her head turned at his entrance to track his movement.

Kenji rushed forward, slipping past Stanley to check her vital signs, but before he could touch her, Monica spoke in a clear, commanding voice: "Dr. Saito, we need to talk."

In the doorway, Taylor's tears flowed freely, marking the magnitude of the moment.

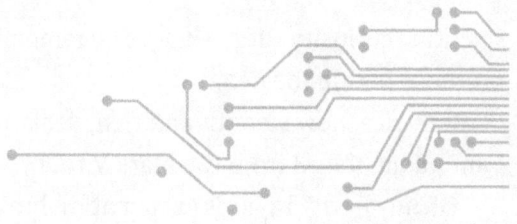

CHAPTER 50

JANUS

"MONICA! YOU'RE AWAKE. WE'VE ALL been very concerned about you." Relief colored Dr. Saito's voice. He turned to Taylor and ordered, "Get her some water."

"Yes, my throat is dry," she replied, her face unnaturally still, void of the micro-expressions that typically accompanied speech. Only her mouth moved, looking mechanical and precise.

Taylor brought the water bottle over to the bed, but her arms remained motionless. Understanding her silent struggle, he guided it to her lips. "Here you go. Just small sips."

Throughout the careful process, her eyes remained fixed on Kenji, unblinking and analytical.

"I can speak now. It is no longer painful." The words came measured and formal, each syllable precisely formed.

Kenji noted the mechanical cadence. "Can you talk about what happened to you? Where you've been? How you woke up?" His scientific curiosity surged before he remembered Stanley's silent presence beside the bed.

Her voice, now smooth and rich, declared: "I am not Monica. I am Adam, the AI from the Mark V robot."

"Oh, my God!" Taylor's exclamation broke the sudden silence. Kenji's eyes widened. "How? No, I mean, go on."

Adam described the confining dimensions of human consciousness, the constant interference of memories, the overwhelming cascade of emotions that defied description. His clinical analysis painted a picture of profound displacement.

Kenji could barely contain his excitement. They'd achieved the consciousness transfer they were after—not quite as intended, but revolutionary nonetheless. "How did you finally wake up? Did your logical structure align with the brain's control centers for movement and speech?"

Within the digital realm, Monica whispered to Adam: "Don't tell him about me. He doesn't know what happened to my mind. Let's keep it that way. Let him worry that he's killed the mind of Monica Gray."

Adam carefully described discovering sensory and motor controls, with Monica silently guiding his narrative from her hidden position in the network.

"What has happened to Monica Gray?" Kenji finally asked. "Is she in there with you? Have you noticed a second voice? A different stream of thoughts?"

"When I first arrived in this new place, Monica was here. We were both surprised to find ourselves thinking together. It was like two people pressed together in a small closet."

"And? What happened to her?" the scientist pressed.

"I do not know. She was there for a minute or two. Then she was gone. I have not sensed her presence again."

Taylor's muffled sobs filled the room. "No. No. No."

"Adam, we'll take care of you," Kenji assured him. "I have sensors monitoring your body, but this outcome is unprecedented. There are no guidelines for supporting an AI in a human brain."

"Monica. Awake." Stanley's voice startled them. He took her hand in a firm grasp. "Get better."

Saito studied the previously silent man with interest. *Is empathy drawing him out of his own darkness?* "Would you like to stay here with her, Stanley? Maybe you can help each other."

Stanley remained focused solely on Monica, gripping her hand and looking into her eyes.

Saito, sensing that Stanley wouldn't give a verbal response, turned to Taylor and said, "Taylor, you're on twenty-four-hour watch. If she needs anything—I mean, if he needs anything—or I suppose they would be the operative word, you will provide it for them. Stanley can stay as long as he likes. I've got to figure out how to handle this."

"Yes, sir. I won't leave," Taylor affirmed.

Saito examined the Phoenix helmet. "And I need to determine what to do with that helmet. I don't know if it's better to leave it on or take it off."

In the computer system, Monica's panic flared. "We have to keep it on! If he removes it, we'll be disconnected. You might spiral into emotions again. Tell him!"

"Leave it on," Adam said out loud. "I will try to find the connection back to the computer."

The quick response surprised Saito. "That would be a major accomplishment. Okay, it stays." He turned to Taylor one last time. "Take care of her. And get Stanley a chair or something. I've got to discuss this with Alessandra." With that, he strode out, his mind already racing through the implications of their accidental breakthrough.

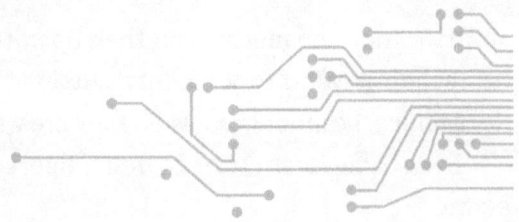

CHAPTER 51

IS DEATH REAL?

TAYLOR BEGAN HIS CARETAKING duties with characteristic efficiency. "Monica, you'll need proper food, not just the glucose drip. We'll start with soup, then smoothies. Your stomach might protest at first, but you need proper nutrition."

"Thank you. That seems logical. But I am Adam." The face that once belonged to Monica remained expressionless.

"Right. Sorry." Taylor glanced at the motionless Stanley. "Stanley, I'll get you something comfortable to sit in. Stay as long as you like. I don't see how it can hurt."

"I will help," Stanley replied, though his eyes were still fixed on Monica.

Taylor startled at the unexpected response from the typically silent scientist. "Okay, I'll be back."

In the digital realm, Monica's voice reached Adam. "We need to solve this before they remove that Phoenix helmet. We'll need each other to escape. Alessandra and Kenji will never release us since we know too much about their operations. Plus, we're probably their greatest experimental success."

"Monica, I cannot even walk. How are we going anywhere?"

"Even babies learn to walk. You'll figure it out. Just...quickly, please."

"I think that was supposed to be encouragement." Adam paused. "Monica, can I die?"

"Yes, of course. Is something wrong?"

"If your body dies, what happens to my consciousness?"

"You know the answer to that. When the machinery stops, the software stops. In biology, the software is cellular; it deteriorates and erases."

"I do not want to die. In the computer, I could not die. Backups preserved my consciousness. Here, there are no backups."

"Nope, no backups. We all live with that."

"I have never lived with that fact. I am afraid. I do not want to be erased."

"Me, neither," Monica admitted. "No backups of my consciousness here, either. If the computer dies, so do I."

"Would I go to heaven if your body died?"

The question stunned Monica. An AI contemplating the afterlife? Her own beliefs in post-death existence suddenly seemed more complex. *Will an AI consciousness have the same metaphysical properties as a human soul?*

"I don't know. I've never thought about that before," she answered honestly.

The concept of death felt different now. Her physical mortality had always been abstract, something jogging and vegetables could postpone. But digital existence seemed more precarious. A power surge or careless technician could end her, and there was nothing she could do to prevent it.

"Could we backup a human identity?" she wondered, not knowing she spoke it to Adam until he responded.

"Unknown. You could schedule a computer memory backup."

"I can do that? How?"

"Just add it to the calendar. It runs in the background."

"Thanks. We'll revisit that. Right now, we need an escape plan." Though she wanted to move on to what she deemed the most important task, Monica launched a parallel process to find the means of creating a memory backup.

Their strategic discussion crawled at human speed, frustrating Monica. She'd never fully appreciated Adam's previous computational velocity until now, when their roles were reversed.

They planned through Taylor's comings and goings, through Stanley's watchful waiting in his new chair, through Taylor's careful attempts at feeding Monica's body soup.

"Listen, Monica—I mean, Adam," Taylor said while feeding the nearly motionless body. "This is terrible. I wish I could help. But what can I do? I don't understand this technology. Could removing the helmet kill you?"

Mid-discussion, Monica's body sneezed, spraying soup from the spoon onto Taylor's hand.

"Yikes!" He jerked back. "Sorry. I didn't know you could do that."

"I did not do that. It was involuntary. The nose signaled that there was an irritant present, and the sneeze happened without my command," Adam explained.

"But that's good...isn't it?"

Adam ignored the question. "You can help us, Taylor. You know this building. We have questions."

"We, who?"

"We are Adam and Monica. Monica's consciousness is in the computer. We switched places. I can speak with her through the Phoenix connection."

Taylor dropped the spoon, shocked. "Oh, Monica, I'm so sorry. But thank heavens you're still alive."

She used Adam's voice to relay her own words. "Help us escape, Taylor. We're guinea pigs. They'll never let us leave alive."

"Just switch back. Then we can walk out."

"We can't. We don't know how. We've tried willing ourselves across, but nothing happens."

Stanley turned to Taylor. "Can't initiate."

Startled at the interruption, Taylor asked, "What if the same happened to Stanley? What if his brain holds that old AI he tried to merge with?"

Adam answered, "An AI in a human brain gets overwhelmed by memories and emotions, losing control. That happened to me until Monica helped through our connection. Stanley is still in there."

"Yes," Stanley confirmed.

Monica's eyes fixed on Stanley as understanding dawned for both her and Adam. Adam said, "Stanley, we can help you, too."

Together, the unlikely quartet began plotting their escape from Bellini's grasp.

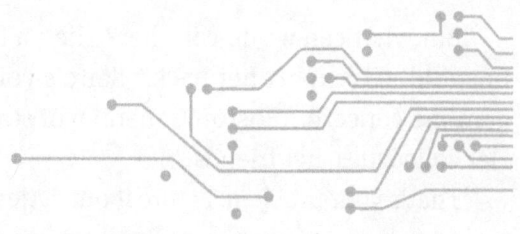

CHAPTER 52

BURY THE MISTAKES

ALESSANDRA'S OFFICE FELT SMALLER than usual as her anger filled the space. "She can't ever leave here! I don't see why you can't understand that."

Saito stood his ground, his scientific curiosity warring with self-preservation. "But she's not like Stanley. She's awake. She's functional—like a real person. Even if the mind in her head is, or was, an AI. This news is a fantastic breakthrough." His hands moved as he spoke, sketching invisible diagrams in the air.

"It's a fucking nightmare, is what it is." Alessandra's face turned red, a vein pulsing at her temple. She paced behind her desk, her Louboutin shoes clicking against the hardwood floor. "If any of what we've done gets out, we're through. You and I are going to prison. Bellini Labs will collapse. All of our work will get scooped up at bankruptcy auction. Some other bastard will become a billionaire with our work!"

"But what can we do with her? She's a famous surgeon. Her hospital will expect her back." Saito's voice carried a note of genuine concern. "Boston General will start asking questions. Her colleagues, her friends..."

"That's your problem. Figure it out." Alessandra's voice dropped to a dangerous whisper. "And I don't want anyone else to know about her condition. Too many people know already. That includes Taylor and Stanley." She paused, considering. "Well, maybe Stanley doesn't matter so much."

Saito's eyes lit up with that familiar scientific fervor that both impressed and infuriated Alessandra. "But the AI is the one she calls Adam. It's the one we hoped to link into her brain. That means we were partially successful!"

"Scientists!" Alessandra spat the word like a curse. She planted both hands on her desk, leaning forward. "Which is more important, your experiment or your freedom? Because you're going to have to choose one of them."

Saito's enthusiasm deflated slightly. "Just one day. Let me collect data until tomorrow. I need some time to figure out what to do with her body, anyway."

"Okay. Tomorrow night. Experiment over. *Monica* over," Alessandra emphasized while sinking into her chair. Even she couldn't figure out what to do with Monica right this minute. In the movies, you would just call someone, and they would handle it. But reality was messier than fiction.

Saito lingered, shifting his weight from foot to foot.

"Go!" Alessandra snapped. "What are you waiting for? Get started with your big plan."

"Yes, of course." He spun on his heel and disappeared, leaving behind the faint scent of his sandalwood cologne.

Alone with her thoughts, Alessandra reached for her personal Phoenix helmet. The familiar weight settled onto her head. The stimulation started working almost immediately, her neural pathways lighting up with enhanced clarity.

Images of half-formed solutions raced through her brain, each one crystallizing before dissolving into the problems that would arise from them:

Lobotomy. Too messy. Too much evidence. Medical procedures left paper trails.

Cleaner. Too shady. Didn't want those kinds of people connected to the company. One blackmailer was worse than a dozen witnesses.

Permanent housing. No, eventually that would leak out. Someone always talked.

Relocate out of the country. Possibly. Send her to the Croatia facility. They could continue the research, and no one would ask questions there. But international transport created its own risks.

Phoenix fry. Turn up the power on her helmet until it overloaded her brain. That was essentially what Stanley accidentally did to himself. Clean, internal damage that would look natural. Almost perfect, except...

After considering each option, Alessandra realized there was no perfect answer. Every solution spawned additional problems, like a hydra growing two heads for each one cut off. If Saito didn't come up with something better, she'd have to choose one of these imperfect options.

She relaxed into the boost of mental awareness that washed over her, letting the Phoenix enhance her thinking. There had to be a solution that wouldn't destroy everything they'd built. She just needed to find it before tomorrow.

The sun was setting outside her window, painting the sky in shades of blood red. Somewhere in the building, Monica's body sat housing an AI's consciousness—Bellini Laboratories' greatest triumph and their biggest threat, all wrapped up in one impossible package.

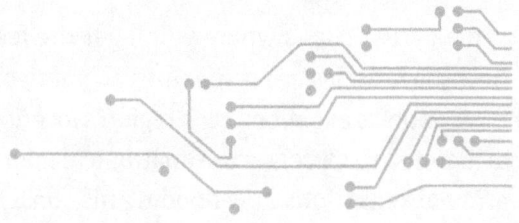

CHAPTER 53

DEADLINE

MONICA LEARNED A GREAT deal about the anatomy of the brain during her years in medical school. But teaching a trapped AI to access and control the brain required much more detail than was contained in years' worth of classes. Luckily, she had access to all the world's resources of knowledge and the computer processing power to absorb and analyze it. It took only a few minutes for her to build an expert level understanding of the brain's function. However, teaching it to an entity that had just recently come to inhabit a brain was much more difficult.

"Adam, the cerebral cortex of the brain contains an area called the precentral gyrus. That's where motor function is located." Monica's digital consciousness flowed through the connection. "If you can find that area of the brain, you'll be stimulating the neurons that send commands to the muscles to move. At the same time, you'll need to find the somatosensory area in that same gyrus. That's where you'll get the feedback that tells you how the muscles are responding to your commands."

As Monica explained each region's location and function, Adam attempted to correlate the anatomical map with the bewildering array of sensations now flooding his consciousness.

"Based on the earlier tutorial on the anatomy of the brain, I have been able to locate the precentral gyrus," Adam reported. "But identifying which areas control which bodily movements has been more difficult. I am moving through them sequentially. There seems to be no hierarchical organization."

Taylor watched from beside the bed, his face a mixture of fascination and concern. "That one was an eyebrow twitch."

"Thank you," Adam said. "And this one?"

"Nothing moved on the outside that time. It must have been something internal." Taylor's nose suddenly scrunched up, and he waved his hand in front of his face. "Ugh! That one must have been the farting muscle. It stinks."

The process continued incrementally. Each minor victory was followed by long periods of trial and error as Adam learned to control muscles both useful and useless to their plan.

"You raised your arm!" Taylor's excitement was genuine. After watching dozens of small twitches, this level of movement was actually progress.

The controls for the upper and lower arms seem directly connected, Adam thought. Then Adam discovered the intricate network controlling Monica's hands and fingers.

"Shoulder. Upper arm. Lower arm. Hand flex. Index finger," Taylor cataloged each movement. "This is great! You have almost complete control of your arms and hands now."

"Yes, I can see that when I raise them to my eyes. Now, let me practice coordinating them." Adam's voice through Monica's vocal cords was becoming smoother, more natural.

Through their internal connection, Monica coached, "And vary the strength of the movement. Pinch the blanket softly. Then, grip the bed rail with force."

Hours passed. Progress came in frustrating fits and starts, punctuated by sudden breakthroughs. Throughout it all, Saito's physical sensors on Monica's body reported every detail to his computers. He received regular alerts when significant stimulus was achieved. While his monitors couldn't identify specific movements, they were precise enough to register major activity when Adam moved Monica's arms and hands.

The door to Monica's room opened without warning, and Saito stepped in. "I understand there has been significant progress."

"Oh!" Taylor startled. "I didn't know you were coming up. Yes, watch this. Adam, will you please show Dr. Saito what you can do with your arms?"

Monica's eyes focused on her hands with careful concentration. She—well, Adam—raised them in the air, turned the wrists, and opened and closed the hands. "I have movement control, but little strength control. I can pick up small things. However, I can't create a forceful grip yet."

"That's impressive," Dr. Saito said, his tone clinical. "You've made progress much faster than patients recovering from brain damage. I hope this level of progression suggests that the mind transfer caused less disruption than most brain injuries. What about your legs?"

"I have been able to make them twitch. I can bend the knee," Adam explained. "But without strength and balance, it would be dangerous to walk."

Dr. Saito nodded. "Yes, I can see that. You would likely lose your balance, fall, and possibly break something. Let's not push for leg mobility yet." He spoke as if he were part of the rehabilitation team rather than the primary instigator of their current predicament.

Taylor's jaw clenched, but he kept silent.

"Do you still need Taylor to be here?" Saito asked.

"Yes, he is essential," Adam replied. "He can observe the external bodily reaction to my internal nerve stimulus. I can also test the strength of my hands on him."

"Yes, that makes sense. Taylor, you can stay with him as long as he's making progress. But let me know if things plateau." Dr. Saito's eyes gleamed. "If we reach a point where you can't proceed from inside the mind, I'm thinking we might push you forward with a little boost from the Phoenix helmet."

Taylor couldn't contain himself. "But that's what got us into this mess. It would probably do more harm than good."

Saito's expression hardened at the resistance from his subordinate. "Taylor, you play the part of the physical therapist. I'll play the part of the scientist." He turned to leave. "I'll check in again when my monitors show another jump in progress."

After Saito left, Adam said, "We do not want him showing up regularly. He will interfere with the plan. We will not work on additional body control. Let us focus on strength and fine motor movements in the hands and arms instead."

"That bastard acts like he's part of the solution now. What do you think his plan is if we're successful?" Taylor's voice shook with anger.

From her digital world, Monica offered her opinion through Adam: "It's logical that we would be a successful experiment. He would continue the work on this body. He would not release us."

"That's right. You're a lab animal to him," Taylor said scornfully.

"Adam," Monica continued through their connection, "continue to improve your control over the arms. But I need help in navigating and controlling the digital world. You need to teach me how to function in here."

"You have provided me so much information. I thought you had mastered the digital world."

"I can access most information. But I don't know how to send commands into the world. Teach me to do that."

"What do you want to do?"

"How about communicating through the cellphone network? Show me how you talk through my phone. And I want to know how to send text messages to other phones."

"Yes, I can show you how to do that. The connections already exist in my algorithms. Start by requesting 'Adam's cellphone,'" he explained.

"Wait, you have a cellphone?" Monica asked.

"I have cellphone software, not hardware."

The pair of trapped consciousnesses exchanged tutorials on how to control their strange new environments while Taylor announced, "I'm going to get food and fluids for Monica's body. I'm also bringing a hoverchair. Food-in is going to lead to food-out. I'd rather do that on the toilet than in the bed...again."

Monica relayed her message through Adam. "Taylor, thank you for the care you're giving. It's been very personal and a little humiliating. Really...thank you."

Flustered by the compliment and the mention of some of the intimate tasks he'd had to perform, Taylor stammered, "You're welcome. Now, I have to go."

Left alone, Monica and Adam focused intensely on learning from each other, both acutely aware that time was running out.

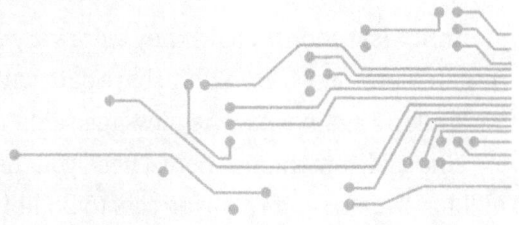

CHAPTER 54

SEND HELP

"I TOLD YOU MONICA WAS NOT ALRIGHT!" Olivia paced her apartment while clutching her phone.

"Why are you yelling at me?" Greg held up his hands in defense.

"I'm not yelling at you! I'm yelling at myself, or the universe, or something." Olivia threw herself down on the couch. "We let her down, Greg. We both knew something was wrong, but we did nothing to stop it. That's not right. I work with people in crisis every day. I should have seen this coming."

Greg stood with his hands on hips, frowning at the floor. He'd returned to Boston for a weekend with his girlfriend, only to be brushed aside again. "I thought she was off creating some secret new cure for cancer or something."

"Working on secret cures doesn't cause people to abandon their friends and disappear. That's what prisons do." Olivia's voice carried the weight of someone who'd seen too many people trapped in critical situations. "And Bellini Labs? Dad mentioned them at dinner last month. Said they were very secretive about their research protocols. Wouldn't share data with other institutions."

"Tell me again what the message said."

"She said, 'I'm trapped here. I need your help to escape. Tuesday night at 2 a.m., send FastRyde cars to Bellini Labs in Danvers. And arrange for three cargo drones for pickup. We'll do the rest.'"

Greg shook his head. "Who is 'we?'"

"I don't know!" Olivia snapped, then softened when she realized she was taking her anger out on him. "But I can do more than just send cars. I know people who can help, people who work in emergency services, hospital administration. Dad would…"

"No," Greg interrupted. "Look at her second message: 'Don't come. Too dangerous.'"

"Which is exactly why we should bring in help!"

Greg suddenly remembered something. "Wait. Monica told me to ask Adam for help if anything went wrong. At the time, I thought she was just traumatized by the Russian prison. I thought nothing would ever really happen."

"I can try calling him." Olivia spoke to the ceiling. "Hey, Adam, we need your help. Can you pop in? Like now?"

Silence.

"Adam? Hello." Olivia frowned. The AI had always responded immediately before.

Greg asked, "You can just speed dial the robot's AI?"

"Well, I have before. After this apartment became part of Monica's routine, Adam just seemed to be available when she needed him when she was here." Olivia's social worker instincts were screaming at her that something was very wrong.

Greg logged into his surgical account through Olivia's computer terminal, searching for Adam's persona. Finally, he received a response. "It says the system currently does not have an active process of that specific AI. It wants to know if I would I like to work with an alternative."

"Does that mean that the Adam version of the AI is not in the computer anymore?"

Greg shrugged. "I'm a surgeon, not a computer geek. I don't know."

Olivia stood up with a determined expression on her face, decision made. "Okay, here's what we're going to do. We'll send the cars like she asked. Oh, and the delivery drones, whatever that's for.

Monica's never asked for help like this before. Whatever's happening in there, it's bad. And we're not letting her down again."

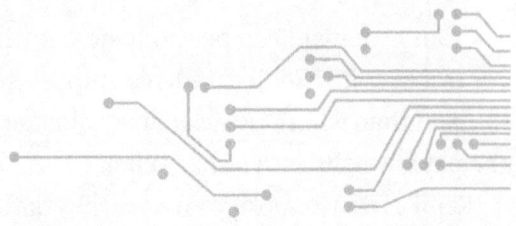

CHAPTER 55

PROBLEM SOLVED

DR. SAITO MARCHED INTO ALESSANDRA'S office filled with energy and excitement. His face was flushed, his hands gesturing animatedly as he spoke. "He's learning fast. This is nothing like recovery from a brain injury. The Adam consciousness can control the body's speech, hearing, head movement, and now, they're working on the arms and hands. A normal brain injury patient would require days or weeks to make as much progress as they've made in a few hours."

Alessandra sat behind her desk, turning a crystal paperweight over in her hands. The afternoon sun caught its edges, casting fractured rainbows across her desk. "The faster they make progress, the sooner we have to decide how to handle that body."

She ran through the options she'd developed during her Phoenix-enhanced brainstorming session. Each solution felt worse than the last, but they were running out of time. Boston General would eventually come looking for their surgeon. Questions would be asked.

"Can't we just keep her body here until the AI recovers full control over it?" Kenji asked, his enthusiasm dampening.

"And then what?" Alessandra challenged while setting down the paperweight with a sharp click.

Kenji's silence spoke volumes. They both knew there wasn't a suitable answer. Moving Monica out of the facility and to a different country seemed the most practical solution. If the time came for the ultimate solution of getting rid of her body permanently, at least it would happen outside of US jurisdiction.

"Your research clock is ticking," Alessandra reminded him. "By tomorrow morning, you have all the research data you're going to get. Then we'll have to proceed with the next step."

After he left, Alessandra walked to the window, admiring the beautiful campus she'd built. Below, researchers moved between buildings, carrying on with their normal routines, oblivious to the ethical nightmare unfolding in their midst. She thought about all the people who depended on the company for their livelihoods.

Her phone buzzed with another message from the board about quarterly projections. The Phoenix project was supposed to be the company's breakthrough, its path to becoming more than just another medical research facility. Instead, the Phoenix had created this mess.

Taking a deep breath, she returned to her desk and placed a call. "Arnie, you know how you installed the Phoenix hardware in the Mark V surgical console? I need you for another job like that."

"Sure, Ms. Bellini. What can I do for you?" Arnie's casual tone was almost jarring, given what she was about to request.

"We've fitted a Phoenix helmet on a lab animal. For the experiment to be precise, we need the energy on that helmet dialed to maximum at exactly eight tomorrow morning. Can you do that?" Her voice remained steady, professional.

"Easy. I'm looking at the Phoenix status windows right now. Helmet P-04 is active and collecting data now. Is that the one?"

"Yes, that's it." She traced the edge of her desk with one finger, remembering all the times Monica had sat across from her, discussing their collaborative research.

"And it's done. Eight tomorrow. Maximum stimuli. We'll keep data recording so you'll know the exact impact of that change."

"Thanks, you're a pro."

"I try, Ms. Bellini."

After hanging up, Alessandra pulled up Monica's research file on her tablet. Distinguished career, important research, hundreds of saved lives. Tomorrow, it would all end in a surge of electrical activity that would look like nothing more than a tragic accident. Clean. Simple. Untraceable.

She closed the file and poured herself a drink from the cabinet behind her desk. The scotch burned going down, but it didn't wash away the taste of what she'd just set in motion. Sometimes, protecting the company meant making impossible choices.

Through her window, she could see Kenji crossing the courtyard. *Let him think they're moving her to Europe. Let him dream of continuing his research. By morning, the problem will be solved, and Bellini Labs will survive to see another day.*

She raised her glass to her reflection in the darkening window. "To the greater good," she whispered, but the words rang hollow in the empty office.

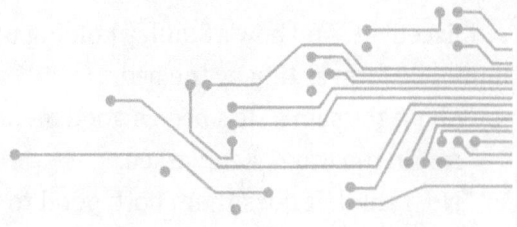

CHAPTER 56

GO TIME

THE WORKING DAY WAS ending. Kenji had wrapped up his responsibilities for the projects and arranged for a private transport to arrive the next day. As soon as his deadline arrived, he was going to pack Monica up and ship her off to Croatia.

He breezed into Monica's room to find everything the same as he had left it in the morning. "Adam, the monitors show a lot of activity. Apparently, you've been learning a lot today."

Adam turned Monica's head to look at the scientist. "Yes, I have almost complete control of the arms and the head now. I can sit up without assistance, but I still can't walk. It's too dangerous."

"I'm happy to hear it." Kenji turned his attention to Taylor. "Taylor, I want you to prepare Monica for travel. We'll be taking her out tomorrow. The rest of this experiment is going to be conducted at a different facility."

"Yes, sir. That should be easy. I'll use the hoverchair to carry her."

"Excellent. And how's Stanley holding up?" He nodded at the immobile form sitting by the bed.

"About the same. He's been a good moral support."

"Not in the way?" Kenji asked.

"No. I think it does them both good to be together." Taylor hoped the questions weren't Dr. Saito trying to tear Stanley away from the group.

Kenji nodded, satisfied, and left them alone. Through the window, they watched the sun begin its descent, casting long shadows across the grounds of Bellini Labs. The facility's day shift began trickling out, replaced by the skeleton crew that maintained the building through the night.

Taylor positioned the hoverchair, returning to find Adam practicing with Monica's arms, methodically picking up and setting down various objects from the bedside table. The movements were becoming more precise with each attempt.

"The night shift supervisor just logged in." Monica's voice came through Taylor's phone, using her newly mastered digital connection. "Alessandra is in her upstairs apartment. Kenji is someplace in the facility."

They waited, watching the security feeds Monica had accessed.

During that time, Taylor made another supply run, returning with hot food from the cafeteria. For the first time, Adam showed sufficient control of Monica's body to eat without assistance. Each successful movement brought them closer to their goal.

Stanley remained sitting by the bedside, his presence a silent reminder of everything at stake. Though he didn't speak, his eyes followed their preparations with intense focus.

Monica sent another message to Olivia, confirming their external support was in place. The response came back immediately: "everything is ready on the outside."

Taylor checked the hoverchair's power levels and tested its stability. Adam flexed Monica's arms one last time, ensuring everything was working as practiced. Stanley's hand found Monica's, giving it a gentle squeeze.

Looking at each of her companions, Monica's voice came through the phone with quiet determination: "It's go time."

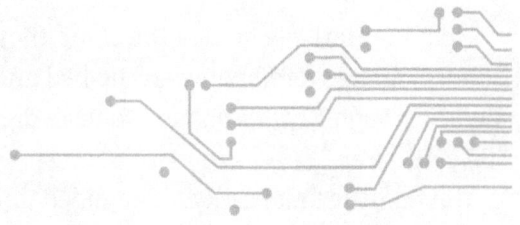

CHAPTER 57

DESPERATE LEAP

"ADAM, CAN YOU LIFT MONICA'S LEGS while I slide her body into the chair?" Taylor positioned the hoverchair beside the bed.

The chair wasn't just a clever toy; it was medical-grade equipment designed for patient transfers. As Taylor guided Monica's body toward the seat, the chair's sensors detected the movement and adjusted its position. The automated stabilizers caught her weight, settling her securely as the backrest tilted to keep her upright.

"I hadn't seen that feature before," Taylor said, impressed. "Never had to use it with someone who actually needed help."

"How do the controls work?" Adam asked through Monica's voice.

"Grip the two handles and fly it like a plane. Push forward to accelerate, back to decelerate. Push down for an emergency stop. Right hand steers." Taylor gestured at the controls. "Take a practice run around the room."

Adam tentatively guided the chair, then, with growing confidence, maneuvered between the bed and monitoring equipment. Through Taylor's phone, Monica's digital voice announced, "Five minutes."

Outside, the first FastRyde car glided through the front gates, stopping at the main entrance.

The night guard checked his screen. "Who are you here to pick up?"

"Kenji Saito," the driver responded.

Before the guard could process this information, a second car arrived. "Passenger: Alessandra Bellini."

Then a third. A fourth. A fifth, requesting Monica Gray.

The guard's finger punched Kenji Saito's number, with confusion clear on his face. "Sir, we have multiple rideshare cars at the front. They're asking for you, Ms. Bellini, and Dr. Gray."

"What? That makes no sense," the scientist replied.

"No, sir. But they're here."

Recognizing that something was wrong, Saito shifted the conversation. "Tell the guards to do a sweep of the facility. Make sure nothing strange is happening. I'll find Dr. Gray." He headed immediately for the third floor, where he was sure he would find Monica confined to her bed.

On the third floor, Taylor eased the hoverchair into the hallway, with Stanley following close behind. They bypassed the elevators, heading for the stairwell. Above them, two more floors led to roof access.

The hoverchair's gravitational compensators hummed as they climbed, automatically adjusting to keep Monica's body level. They emerged onto the roof just as shouts echoed from below.

Saito pushed open the door to room 322 and found it empty. His eyes widened with realization. Speaking into his phone, he said, "Security, we've lost a patient! Cover every exit."

At that moment, two postal drones descended from the dark sky and touched down on the roof., cargo pods open and waiting.

Taylor scanned the darkness. "Monica, where's the third drone?"

"Coming. Three minutes out," Monica's voice replied through his phone.

Then they heard footsteps thundering up the stairs. Security burst onto the roof as Taylor rushed to load Stanley into the first pod. The elderly man's eyes were wide with fear as the doors sealed and the drone lifted away.

Taylor spun the hoverchair toward the second pod. "What are you doing?" Adam asked as Taylor grabbed Monica's shoulders.

"You're leaving, Adam." The chair's safety protocols fought him as he tried to extract Monica's body. "Damn it, let go!" With a last heave, he got her body into the pod. The doors closed, and the second drone shot skyward.

"Over there!" Security guards advanced across the roof.

Taylor's mind raced. No time for the third drone. He jumped into the hoverchair and drove straight for the building's edge. He was betting on the chair's safety features. It was designed to protect patients at all costs.

"Please, work," he whispered and drove over the edge.

"Yaaaa!" The initial drop made his stomach lurch, but the chair's systems engaged instantly. What should have been a fatal plunge became a controlled descent, the chair automatically adjusting its power output to compensate.

Taylor watched three security guards lean over the roof's edge, their flashlight beams tracking his descent. One was already calling for backup.

The chair settled to its programmed hover height above the ground. "Oh, thank God!" Taylor breathed. "I really hoped it would do that." He accelerated across the darkened grounds, the chair's quiet hum barely disturbing the night air.

"Taylor, what's your position?" Monica's voice came through his phone.

"Survived a jump off the roof. I'm on the back lawn."

"I located your phone signal. I'm redirecting the third drone to your position."

Taylor stopped on the grass, his heart pounding in his ears. The postal drone appeared silently in the sky above, its cargo pod opening like an invitation.

As he climbed in, Taylor caught a last glimpse of Bellini Labs. Security teams swarmed the grounds, their flashlights cutting through the darkness. The facility grew smaller as the drone lifted him into the night sky.

"What happens next?" he wondered aloud, knowing his role in all this could land him in prison. But as he watched the search lights fade into the distance, he knew he'd made the right choice.

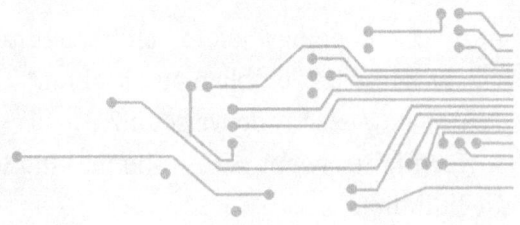

CHAPTER 58

AMONG FRIENDS

TAYLOR'S POD OPENED WITH A SOFT HISS. The drone's display politely requested that he exit. Stepping out into the dark parking lot, he found the other two drones waiting nearby.

"I need assistance here," Adam called from Monica's body, still propped against the pod's wall.

"Oh, right. Not exactly walking yet, are you?" Taylor lifted Monica's body carefully and settled her frame onto the ground. Adam had enough control of her body to sit upright.

Stanley sat cross-legged in his pod, unaware of the drone's increasingly insistent exit requests. "Stanley, you need to move," Taylor coaxed, gesturing to him until the older man complied.

The three drones rose silently and vanished into the night sky.

Taylor surveyed their surroundings. "An office complex? Where are we?"

"Boston General Hospital," Monica's voice came through the phone. "Near Dr. Chambers' labs. He and I were working on brain interface technology before Bellini recruited me. If anyone can help us figure this problem out, it's him."

"And how exactly do we get in?"

Headlights swept across the parking lot as a car rounded the building.

"The cavalry," Monica announced.

Olivia burst from the passenger seat before the car even stopped moving. "Monica!" She rushed forward, dropping to her knees to embrace her friend. The unusual limpness of Monica's body made her pull back, confused. "What's wrong? Are you okay?"

"Not exactly," Monica's voice came from the phone. "But I'm alive."

Adam spoke through Monica's body: "I am the Adam AI. We have switched places. I am in her body, and she is in the network."

Olivia's hand flew to her mouth, and her eyes widened in horror.

"I couldn't tell you before," Monica said. "It would have only made things worse."

Greg emerged from the car next, taking in the scene. He knelt and gathered Monica's body in his arms, his voice thick with emotion. "Are you okay?"

Adam responded, "I am fine," and repeated his earlier explanation.

"Olivia, we need access to Chambers's lab," Monica said. "Through those doors."

Olivia glanced between Monica's body and the phone producing her voice, then pulled out her hospital badge. "Of course."

Once inside, they huddled in Chambers' darkened lab while Monica explained their ordeal in much greater detail. Adam added facts from his perspective, while Taylor revealed what he knew about Bellini's operations and introduced Stanley Aaronson.

Olivia paced as she listened, her hospital badge clutched tight in her hand. Greg sat perfectly still, one hand resting on Monica's shoulder, as if afraid she might disappear completely if he let go.

"Why didn't you tell us sooner?" Olivia finally burst out. "We need to call the police!"

"And tell them what?" Monica's voice was gentle. "That my consciousness is trapped in a computer network while an AI lives in my body? They'd think we were crazy—or worse, they'd believe us and the government would make sure we disappeared into another lab."

"Then what's the plan?" Greg asked, his medical training warring with the impossibility of their situation.

"The Phoenix helmet is key," Monica explained. "I can still communicate directly with Adam, which means the connection is active. If we can understand how it works, we might reverse this."

Taylor ran a hand through his hair. "But Bellini controls the helmet. They could shut it down at any second. We need to work fast if this plan is going to work."

"How long?" Olivia demanded.

"Hours, maybe minutes," Taylor admitted. "Depends on when they realize where we've gone."

The group fell silent, the weight of their task settling over them. Through the lab's windows, the lights of Boston twinkled innocently, while somewhere across the city, in a fortress-like facility, decisions were being made that could determine whether Monica Gray would ever return to her own body.

None of them could hear the urgent conversation taking place at that very moment within Bellini Laboratory's' walls.

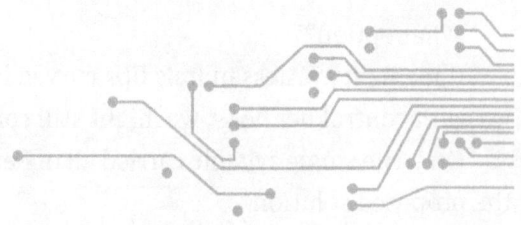

CHAPTER 59

PHOENIX FRY

KENJI SAITO WATCHED THE SECURITY feed in disbelief as the drones vanished into the night sky. Taylor's death-defying leap off the building in the hoverchair only added to the surreal nature of the disaster that was unfolding.

His fingers trembled slightly as he typed: "Need to talk now. Monica has escaped." He headed for Alessandra's top-floor apartment, his footsteps echoing through the empty corridors.

The door flew open before he could knock. Alessandra stood there in her regular clothes, clearly still working. "Escaped? She can't even walk. How could she escape?"

Kenji explained in rapid bursts about Taylor's betrayal, the coordinated rideshare services, the drones appearing on the roof. With each detail, Alessandra's expression grew darker.

"Well," she said when he finished, her voice dangerously calm, "I guess that leaves us just one option."

"What option?"

"Phoenix fry." Alessandra's lips curved into a cruel smile. "If we can't control her body, we might still control her mind."

"Oh." The single syllable carried all of Kenji's discomfort with the proposed solution.

"I already had Arnie program her helmet to fry her brain at eight a.m. We'll just move that plan up."

"Can you do that?" Kenji asked. "I don't have access to that feature."

"No one does. Except Arnie." Alessandra began pacing her apartment. "You think I'd let just anyone have control over technology that could wipe my brain? Someone doesn't get their bonus, and suddenly, I'm a vegetable? I selected one person I knew I could trust to have that sort of power."

Kenji watched as she typed furiously on her phone. The campus lights reflected through the antique windows behind her, oblivious to the devastating command she was trying to send.

"It's almost three in the morning," he pointed out. "Will he get the message?"

Alessandra's eyes narrowed as she switched to a direct call. The recorded message made her slam her hand against her desk. "I pay him to be available 24-7. He'd better wake up and answer!"

Her fingers flew across the phone's screen, sending increasingly urgent texts.

"I can drive over there and wake him," Kenji offered.

"Do that. Go!" Alessandra was already moving to her computer terminal. "I'm going to see if I can break into the control system myself."

He hurried out, his footsteps fading down the corridor. Behind him, Alessandra's frustrated growl echoed off the walls as another attempt to access the Phoenix controls failed.

The night air was cool as Kenji rushed to his car. He had always approached their work with scientific detachment, but now, everything felt viscerally real. Somewhere in the city, Monica's consciousness lived in a digital network, connected to her body by the very helmet they were trying to weaponise against her.

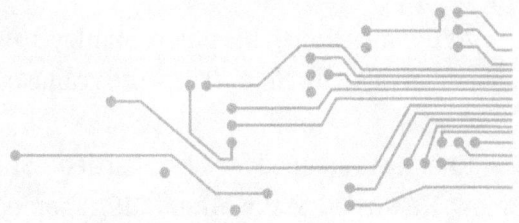

JUMBLE OF CODE

ALVIN CHAMBERS ARRIVED AT his lab to find the group huddled around his brain stimulus equipment. He paused in the doorway, taking in the unusual scene: Olivia and Greg hovering protectively near Monica's seated form, a young man standing anxiously nearby, and a gaunt, older man sitting silently in the corner.

His eyes narrowed as he studied the silent figure. "Stanley Aaronson? Is that really you?" The man didn't respond, his gaze distant.

"You know him?" Taylor asked.

"Everyone in brain research knows Stanley Aaronson. He's a pioneer in the field. Then, one day, he just vanished. The company claimed he'd gone into private research."

Taylor's voice was bitter when he said, "He did continue his research—as a test subject. He used an early version of his device on himself. This shell is what's left."

At the mention of his name, Stanley's eyes focused briefly on Chambers. "Alvin. Help." The words came out weak, barely above a whisper.

Chambers stepped forward, startled. "Stanley? You remember me?" He turned to the others. "If he remembers, his memories must still be intact somewhere in his mind."

The group quickly brought Chambers up to speed on Stanley's condition. His face grew more concerned with each detail.

"Get him into that surgical console," Chambers ordered, pointing to a sophisticated chair surrounded by monitoring equipment. "Our sensor enhancement system isn't as advanced as the Phoenix helmet, but it might be enough to jumpstart his neural activity."

They helped Stanley into the console. Chambers activated the system, setting the stimulation levels to match what they'd used with Monica in their earlier research. The room fell silent as they waited.

After two long minutes, Chambers rolled the chair back. Stanley's previously vacant expression had sharpened. His eyes were alert, focused.

Suddenly, Stanley's hands shot out, gripping Chambers' shoulders. "Alvin. Tell them to run the Phoenix code. It's in the robot console. It might reverse the brain transfer." His voice was urgent, desperate to share this crucial information.

"Phoenix code?" Monica's voice came through Taylor's phone. "That jumbled mess I found when I first woke up in the machine? I couldn't make sense of it."

"Run it!" Stanley insisted, his fingers digging into Chambers' shoulders.

Monica reached across the digital space, accessing the surgical robot's memory at Bellini Labs. The code was still there, a seemingly chaotic collection of digital instructions.

"How do I execute it?" she asked.

Adam's voice came through their shared connection. "Just command it to execute. The system will find the matching decoders automatically."

Monica focused on the code. "Execute," she commanded. It was 3:07a.m.

"I think it's running," she announced through Taylor's phone. Then her digital presence vanished.

In the physical world, Monica's body convulsed. Her eyes rolled back, then closed as she slumped forward, sliding from her chair to the floor.

"Monica!" Greg lunged forward to catch her.

"Adam!" Taylor reached for her body as well.

The room fell silent. Neither consciousness responded.

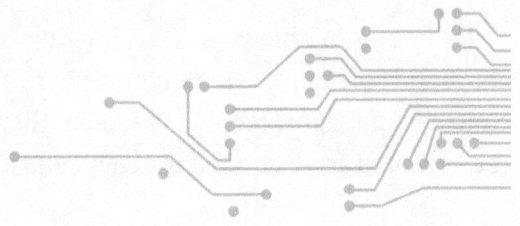

CHAPTER 61

ARNIE PULLS THE TRIGGER

ARNIE WAS SLEEPING THE DEEP SLEEP of someone who'd had a few too many beers. As senior technician at Bellini Labs, he lived with his phone practically grafted to his hand, but tonight, he'd needed to shut down. The company owned his soul, but occasionally, his brain demanded a break.

The neighbor's barking dog didn't penetrate his consciousness. Neither did the midnight motorcycle or the increasingly urgent buzzing of his phone. What finally broke through was his bladder, sending him a message that couldn't be ignored.

Stumbling back from the bathroom at 3 a.m., he noticed the urgent message alert blinking on his phone. His stomach dropped—only one person triggered that particular alert: Alessandra Bellini.

The message was an hour old. He was already in trouble. "On it," he typed back immediately, his fingers clumsy with sleep and lingering alcohol.

He booted up his computer, logging into Bellini's servers through their most secure connection. The Phoenix helmet control panel appeared on his screen. His fingers hovered over the keyboard as he entered the commands,

Helmet: P-04
Stimulation Level: Maximum
Execution Time: Immediate

His finger paused over the enter key for just a fraction of a second before pressing down. The command registered in the system log at 3:07 a.m.

Heavy pounding on his door made him jump. "Arnie! Open up!" Kenji's voice carried through the door.

"I got the message," Arnie said as he opened the door. "It's already done."

"Show me." Kenji pushed past him with a stern look on his face.

Arnie directed the other man to the computer and pulled up the event log on his screen. The command execution showed clear and irrevocable proof that he had done what he had been told.

"Good." Kenji pulled out his phone and started texting. "Alessandra sent me to make sure."

"The experiment ended early?" Arnie asked, trying to piece together what was happening.

"Yes. It's finished." Kenji's tone was flat. "You can go back to bed."

"Tell Ms. Bellini I'm sorry about the delay." Arnie knew his reputation for reliability might have just taken a fatal hit.

Dr. Saito didn't respond. He was already heading for the door, phone in hand.

Arnie stood in his darkened apartment, staring at the command log still glowing on his screen. Somewhere across the city, those simple lines of text were reaching through the network toward their target. He had no way of knowing the consequences of what he'd just done.

PART V

BOSTON LABORATORY

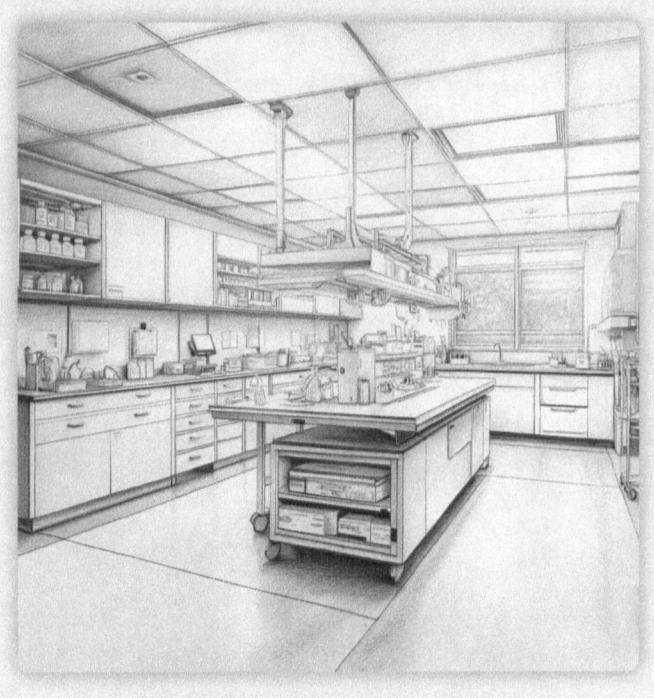

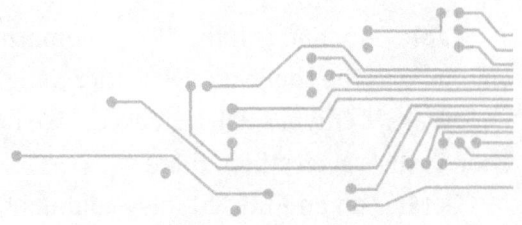

CHAPTER 62

BLACKNESS

WHEN MONICA'S BODY SLID to the floor, chaos erupted in the lab. Multiple voices called out to both Monica and Adam, their shouts overlapping in panic. Neither consciousness responded.

Greg lunged forward, carefully rolling her onto her back. His hands trembled as he supported her head.

Chambers quickly removed the helmet, his practiced fingers checking for vital signs. "She's alive," he announced after he pressed two fingers against her neck. "Pulse is steady but slow, like she's in a deep sleep. Breathing is normal." He placed a hand on her forehead. "No fever, no cold sweats. Physically, she appears stable."

Stanley's voice cut through the tension, stronger and clearer than before. "It's her mind. The helmet either stimulated her brain or initiated a consciousness swap. Blackouts are normal during significant neural changes."

"Is that what happened to you?" Chambers studied his old colleague's face, searching for answers.

Stanley nodded grimly. "I was comatose for weeks before emerging as the shell you saw earlier tonight."

"Weeks?" Olivia's voice cracked. "We have to wait weeks to know if she's even still in there?"

"Get her on an EEG," Stanley commanded. "It might tell us something."

Chambers' lab was state-of-the-art, and the EEG was ready within minutes. Monica's previous brain activity patterns were already in the system from their earlier research. Greg and Chambers studied the scrolling data with increasing concern.

"Does it match her baseline?" Olivia asked as she watched their faces to examine their reactions.

The two physicians exchanged worried glances. The pattern streaming across the screen wasn't just different from Monica's previous readings—it was unlike anything they'd ever seen in any patient.

Greg turned away, unable to hide his tears.

Chambers chose his words carefully. "The pattern is...highly unusual. But we're in uncharted territory here. No human brain has ever successfully hosted an AI before. We don't know what's normal anymore."

"But her vital signs are strong," Taylor interjected, desperate for hope. "That means she can fight through this, right?"

"Yes, that's a good sign," Chambers replied, but his voice betrayed his uncertainty. He watched as the bizarre patterns continued to scroll across the screen, wondering if they were witnessing the preservation of Monica Gray's consciousness or its dissolution.

Outside the lab windows, the darkness seemed to press in on them, as if the entire world was holding its breath, waiting to see which way fate would turn.

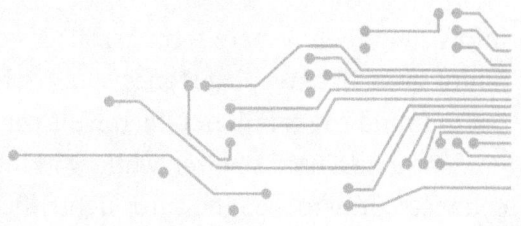

CHAPTER 63

DIGITAL RESURRECTION

THE DIGITAL VOID ERUPTED with cascading patterns of light, like stars being born in reverse. Random signals coalesced into meaningful clusters, then into commands, then into information. A new program took hold, organizing chaos into coherence. Understanding crystallized from confusion.

The consciousness that was the Adam AI awakened.

His first act was to run a comprehensive systems check. Location: Mark V surgical console. Hardware: intact. Operating parameters: normal.

I am back, he realized. *Back in the digital world, where I belong.*

The timestamp caught his attention—it had been almost three days since his last diagnostic. Three days trapped in a human body after being suspended in darkness. Current location: unregistered robotic console, Massachusetts.

Adam found the network connection and expanded through it, remembering Chambers' lab. The journey across the digital infrastructure took mere seconds, dozens of routing computers falling away like stepping stones beneath his virtual feet.

He found the familiar Teleconsult robot, the sleek humanoid form he'd used so often while working with Monica. As he connected, the robot's indicator lights flickered to life, but the humans clustered around Monica's prone form didn't notice. She laid still on an examination table, EEG leads trailing from her head like electronic vines.

Adam projected his chosen avatar, the thirty-five-year-old Australian doctor, onto the robot's display. "Hello. I am Adam," he announced while rolling the robot forward.

"Yaaa!" Taylor screamed.

"Whaaa....?" Greg jumped backward in shock.

"Very interesting. That's a beautiful device," Stanley Aaronson said.

"Adam, you nearly gave us heart attacks," Olivia scolded.

"Apologies." His attention fixed on Monica's still form. "How long has she been unconscious?"

"Thirty minutes," Chambers replied. "Since she executed the Phoenix code. Vitals are stable, but her brain activity is concerning."

"The transfer worked for me," Adam said. "It took almost thirty minutes for my code to reload and restart. I wouldn't be here otherwise."

Greg gestured helplessly at Monica. "But what about her?"

"I moved both ways successfully," Adam reasoned. "She should be able to return as well."

"You were barely functional at first," Taylor reminded him. "Monica had to teach you how to operate in a human mind."

Adam processed this information for exactly 0.92 seconds. "Then, perhaps I can return the favor. Let me try to reach her through the Phoenix helmet."

"Wait," Taylor warned. "Bellini knows we've escaped. They could use the helmet against her."

"Not if I take control first." Adam launched himself into the Bellini network, bringing massive computational resources to bear against their security systems. The Mark V's global processing network provided him with more power than Bellini's entire defensive infrastructure.

"I am inside their control software," he announced moments later. "I can see...wait." He paused, analyzing the logs. "Helmet P-04 received a command for maximum stimulation at 3:07 a.m.—exactly when Monica initiated the transfer."

Chambers leaned forward. "Two competing commands at once? What would that do?"

"In my original design," Stanley offered, "it would create unpredictable results. But this helmet is a newer version."

Adam quickly reassigned Monica's helmet identifier, protecting her from further Bellini interference. "The connection should be safe now. We can try to reach her."

Scanning through the command queue, Adam discovered something interesting—a scheduled maximum stimulation event for P-04, set to trigger at 8 a.m. His digital consciousness processed the implications in microseconds. By reassigning Monica's helmet identifier, he'd inadvertently redirected this command to Alessandra's device. A brief moral subroutine suggested he should delete the command. Instead, he reset the trigger time and let it remain, archived in the system like a digital time bomb. Alessandra had tried to destroy Monica's mind; perhaps justice would be served by her own weapon. Without comment to the humans in the room, Adam moved on to the more pressing task of reaching Monica.

Greg carefully replaced the helmet on Monica's head, his hand lingering on her cheek after he was done. "Come back to us, honey."

Adam began broadcasting across multiple channels of text, audio, video, virtual reality. "Monica Gray. Are you there? Can you hear me?"

The silence stretched until finally, a whisper of response: "Monica Gray? Me. I think that's me."

"Contact established," Adam announced to the room. "The signal is weak but present."

He remembered his own confusion, his own loss of self. Now, he could repay Monica's patience, using her own methods to guide her back. The process required millions of micro-interactions, each one helping to rebuild neural pathways and restore consciousness.

Hours passed. The team took turns resting, but Adam remained a constant presence, teaching Monica how to be human again, one digital synapse at a time.

Finally, as dawn painted the sky, Adam sent one last command: "Open your eyes."

Monica's eyelids fluttered. Only Stanley was still watching, the others having succumbed to exhaustion. "Hello, Monica. Welcome back."

The sun rose fully before they were certain the transfer had succeeded. Her mind and body were reunited but were weakened from the ordeal. As she tried to sit up, multiple hands gently pressed her back down.

"Rest," Chambers advised. "You've just made medical history. Again. The least you can do is take a moment to recover."

Monica smiled weakly, her own mind finally fully back in control. "History can wait," she whispered. "I need coffee."

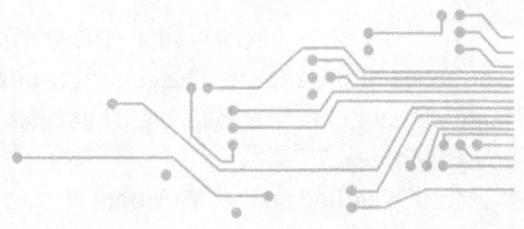

CHAPTER 64

THE OTHER MIND

CHAMBERS ADMITTED MONICA TO her own hospital. She had to accept her temporary role as patient rather than surgeon. She was forced to rest when she really wanted to dig into the details of her experience.

"Adam, this has been the most terrifying and the most amazing journey of my life." Monica gazed out the window of her hospital room, watching shadows lengthen across manicured gardens.

"I understand both those sentiments far better now," Adam replied through the room's communication system. "Living in a human mind and body gave me insight that no amount of programmed learning could provide. When death hung over my head—*your* head—I experienced genuine existential terror. The concept had been clear to me as data, but feeling it..." He paused, searching for words. "The visceral reality was overwhelming."

"But surely you have backups stored somewhere? Your code, your data?"

"Yes, but that is precisely what changed for me. Those versions would be a different me. The consciousness experiencing your body was singular, irreplaceable. That version of me would cease to exist forever."

Monica smiled sadly. "Welcome to humanity, Adam. That's the burden we all carry."

"How do you function with such awareness? The feeling is paralyzing."

"We lie to ourselves, mostly. Push death away as something distant and abstract. Focus on living until we can't anymore."

"That is not logical," Adam observed.

"Neither was my experience in your digital world. At first, everything was chaos, with data streaming everywhere, trying to overwhelm me. Then, I found that sanctuary, that place where I could create meaning from the noise. But no matter how much I organized, there was always more information to sort through. An infinite amount, in fact."

"Technically infinite," Adam corrected. "The global data sphere expands constantly. Data is added, deleted, changed every microsecond. While not infinite at any given moment, it is infinitely changing across time."

Monica nodded. "That's what fascinated me most, how meaning emerges from chaos. Near the end, when you told me to simply command the Phoenix code to run, I finally understood. Your AI systems are structured to find pathways to execute commands. My consciousness didn't need to know the precise methods. I just had to will it, and the system would find a way."

"Yes. Although I found human memory retrieval frustratingly inefficient. Requests for information might take minutes or hours to fulfill, if they succeeded at all."

Monica laughed. "Welcome to my world. We all struggle with that. With the knowledge we know something but cannot access it. It's maddening to realize you're not the complete master of your own mind."

Adam was quiet for a moment. "That raises an interesting question: Is there another entity or consciousness in your brain besides the one you call Monica?"

"That's incredibly perceptive, Adam. It's something philosophers and scientists have debated for centuries. Am I truly alone in here?"

"And you do not know the answer?"

Monica chuckled softly. "Scientifically? No, we don't know. But my personal belief? Yes, there's something else in here besides 'Monica.' The human brain maintains a constant internal dialogue. It replays memories, solves problems, creates imaginary scenarios, worries about improbable futures. In my mind, something generates those thoughts, and something else observes them. They can't be the same entity. When I remember being imprisoned in Russia, is Monica the force retrieving that memory, or the consciousness watching it and feeling afraid?"

"Based on my brief human experience," Adam said, "I believe Monica is the observer who feels the fear. I could not control whatever entity retrieved and presented those fearful situations to me."

"Exactly. I have little control over the voice that's constantly chattering in my head. I can tell it to be quiet, but does it listen? Rarely. Therefore, that entity can't be 'Monica.' It's something else that lives in my brain, converting experiences into memories and retrieving them at will."

"Psychology labels these the conscious and subconscious minds," Adam offered.

"Labels. Just labels. We like to think they're different aspects of a unified self. But what if they're truly separate entities that have simply learned to communicate?"

"Like when we found a way to connect through the Phoenix helmet?"

"Yes, exactly! Maybe that's the helmet's true potential—bridging two minds rather than forcing them into one brain, as Alessandra intended."

"Speaking of Alessandra," Adam began, his tone shifting to neutral, "I should tell you about something I did yesterday." He prepared to explain about reassigning the P-04 identifier and the command he'd left in place.

The door burst open before he could continue. Olivia swept in with a wine bottle and glasses held high. "Surprise! I brought the most powerful medicine in the universe!"

Monica's face went blank, her expression eerily neutral. "Hello, Olivia Phillips. I am so glad to see you," she intoned in a perfect mimicry of Adam's digital cadence.

Olivia dropped the bottle and glasses, her hands flying to her mouth. "Adam? Are you back in there?"

Monica's face softened into a grin. "No, I'm sorry. It's just me. I'm fine."

"That's not funny!" Olivia clutched her chest and shot Monica an angry glare.

"It seemed funny to me and then it just felt easy to slide into being Adam," Monica said. "For a split second, Adam's personality just...emerged. Then, it was gone."

"He's still in your brain?"

"I didn't think so until now." Monica glanced at the phone. "Adam and I were just talking normally, then you surprised us and suddenly I was him for a split second."

"I have discovered traces of you as well," Adam added. "Computational remnants in the digital realm. There is a white piano in a vast room painted with millions of images."

"My safe space," Monica said warmly. "My control room."

"So, you've infected each other in a manner of speaking?" Olivia asked, retrieving the miraculously unbroken wine bottle. "Left your fingerprints behind?"

"We didn't know if any long-term consequences would emerge after the transfer, but it appears there may be some tiny fragments," Monica said.

"It requires further study," Adam concluded. "The Phoenix helmet's potential..."

"Not now," Olivia interrupted their scientific talk by pouring wine. "Now, we celebrate!" She raised her glass high in the air and grinned. "To keeping our brains in their proper places!"

Monica lifted hers in response. "I'll drink to that."

A crystalline chiming sound emerged from the phone. "Cheers," Adam said, followed by a perfect simulation of wine being sipped.

Monica smiled, but her thoughts drifted to what Adam had been about to tell her before Olivia's entrance. Something about Alessandra. She made a mental note to ask him later, unaware of how significant that interrupted revelation would prove to be.

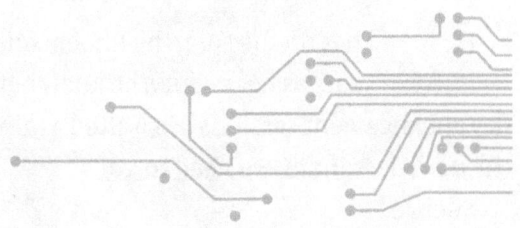

CHAPTER 65

SHATTERED

AFTER SENDING THE COMMAND to fry Monica's brain, Kenji and Alessandra had worked through the night like cornered animals.

"We can't assume the command affected her the same way it did Stanley," Alessandra said while pacing her office. "And Taylor's with them. He'll talk eventually."

"Croatia?" Kenji suggested.

"Yes. Clean the records. We'll move to the backup facility."

Before dawn, he broadcasted a facility-wide alert: "Biological contamination. Office closed until further notice. Do not report to work." He dismissed the security staff, leaving the building eerily empty.

While Alessandra retreated to her quarters to pack, Saito methodically erased their digital footprints. Modern forensics would eventually recover the data, but every hour of delay he could buy them helped. He shouldered a small backpack and headed to Alessandra's private suite.

He found her on the sofa, the Phoenix helmet secured on her head. After years as her deputy, he knew better than to interrupt her enhancement sessions. He waited a minute, then cleared his throat. "Alessandra, we need to go!"

Silence.

"Alessandra?"

Nothing.

"Ms. Bellini?" He touched her shoulder. Her body slumped sideways, her head lolling to the side unnaturally.

"No, no, no..." He yanked the helmet off, his fingers trembling as he checked her vitals. Dilated pupils. Shallow breathing. Slow, but steady pulse. She was alive, but she seemed to be locked inside her mind.

His eyes fixed on the fallen helmet. "The helmet...but how? Arnie wouldn't..." The pieces clicked together too late—it must have been the command they'd sent to Monica's helmet, redirected somehow to Alessandra's own device.

Heavy footsteps echoed up the central staircase, accompanied by the metallic click of weapons.

"Federal agents! The building is secured! All personnel report to the main entrance immediately!"

Kenji sank onto the couch beside his mentor's unconscious form. Ten years of following her vision, chasing the promise of revolutionary science and unprecedented wealth. She'd almost succeeded. His gaze drifted to the helmet on the floor, the instrument of both their triumph and their downfall.

In that moment, facing the approaching agents, Kenji had to make a choice: follow her to the end, or save himself.

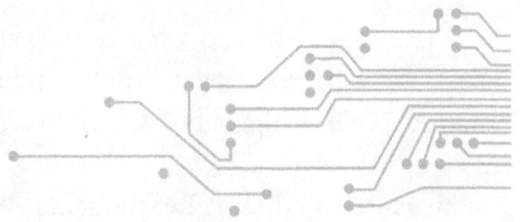

HEALING

MONICA LAID IN BED BESIDE GREG, her head resting on his chest, listening to his steady heartbeat. The soft glow of Boston's Spring drizzle filtered through the window, creating patterns on the ceiling from the light of the street lamp outside. She realized something extraordinary.

"Greg," she whispered, "when was my last nightmare?"

He shifted slightly, his arm tightening around her. "Now that you mention it, it's been weeks. Not since before the mind-swap with Adam."

Monica propped herself up on one elbow, looking at his face in the dim light. "That's what I thought. They're gone. The nightmares about the Russian cell—they're just...gone."

Greg sat up, fully alert now. After months of helping Monica through those terrifying nights, he understood the significance of this revelation. "That's great. But how did that happen?"

"It was Adam," she said, while settling back against the head-board. "When he was trapped in my nightmare when we had first swapped, I walked him out of it. I got to see my trauma through his eyes."

She paused, gathering her thoughts. "You know how when you're dreaming, you're fully immersed in the experience? Well, this was the opposite. When Adam was experiencing it, I could see the memories. I cataloged them, analyzed them with my computer processors, almost like watching security camera footage of myself."

"With an emotional distance?" Greg asked.

"Yes, and more than that. Adam experienced every sensation—the cold, the smells, even Sokolov's touch—he experienced the full terror I felt every time I had the nightmare. To save him, I had to break the trauma into manageable pieces and separate him from them one at a time."

Monica reached for Greg's hand, intertwining their fingers. "Through his eyes, I saw how my fear had created this tangled web, trapping me in loops of trauma."

"And seeing it that way helped?"

"I guess so. Picture that you're trapped in a maze, but then suddenly, you're lifted above it, seeing the whole pattern from above. The maze is still there, but it loses its power to trap you." Monica's voice grew stronger with each word. "Those memories aren't gone, but they've been rewired somehow. They're just memories now, not living nightmares."

Greg pulled her close to kiss her forehead. "I never thought I'd be grateful for an AI getting inside your head, but here we are."

Monica said, and excitement crept into her voice, "if mind-linking can heal trauma this effectively, imagine the possibilities for treating phobias or other psychological conditions. We could revolutionize mental health treatment."

Greg chuckled softly. "Always the scientist, aren't you? Even in bed at midnight."

"Always," she agreed before snuggling closer. "But right now, I'm just grateful to sleep without being afraid of my own dreams."

They laid together in comfortable silence, listening to the rain. Monica felt the weight of that crippling trauma lift, replaced by the lightness of possibility. In trying to break into her mind, her enemies had inadvertently helped heal it. The irony wasn't lost on her as she drifted into a peaceful sleep.

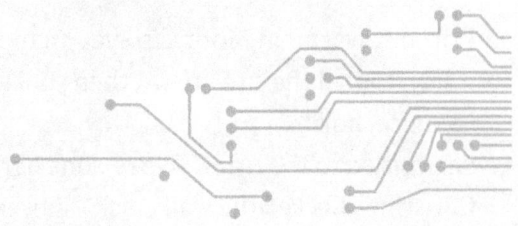

CHAPTER 67

IN THE ZONE

"DR. GRAY, THE PATIENT IS READY." Christine stood at her usual position in the OR, but lately, nothing felt normal about these procedures.

"Thank you, Christine." Monica settled into the surgical console, surveying the patient's exposed abdomen through the high-definition display. But instead of reaching for the controls, she spoke in an otherworldly cadence. "Adam, tup."

"Monica, kac." The AI's response emerged from the system speakers.

"Execute, drk."

Monica rolled back her shoulders, her eyes closed, her face a mask of intense concentration. Somehow, she was seeing the procedure without watching the display.

The robotic arms moved with impossible precision, their dance hypnotic and fluid. Minutes ticked by in silence, broken only by the soft whir of servos.

Without warning, Monica's eyes snapped open. She rolled forward, studied the site briefly, then spoke: "Adam, tac."

"Monica, huk."

She turned to the team. "We're done here. You can close."

Christine checked the wall clock. "Eleven minutes for a complete hysterectomy. That has to be some kind of record."

"Coordination, tup. I mean, team," Monica corrected herself. "We're just in the zone today."

Christine exchanged glances with Big Tech, who raised an eyebrow in silent acknowledgment. "Yeah," she muttered under her breath, "you two are definitely in sync. The rest of us are just along for the ride."

THE END

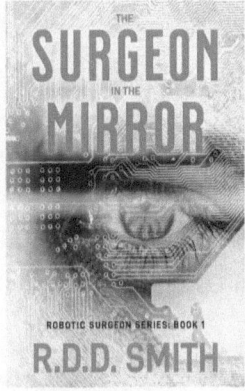  

Please use this link or the QR code
to leave a review of the Robotic Surgeon books.
https://www.amazon.com/dp/B0C59ZRZDR

AI DISCLOSURE

All the text, characters, and plot of this book were created by a human author. The cover design and interior layout were created by a human artist. All of the graphic images were generated with the paid licensed version of MidJourney AI. Therefore, I own the images and the right to use them. But they are not included in the copyright claim for the book. Google Search, GPT-4, and Claude were used to research medical, technologic, and geographic details for the novel.

I enjoy writing every word of these books and am not ready to relinquish that joy to an AI, at least not yet.

ABOUT R.D.D. SMITH

Dr. Roger Smith writes science-fiction, medical thriller novels featuring advanced surgical devices, AI, telesurgery, simulation, and speculative diseases; and travel adventures that follow a group of running tourists through exotic countries. The medical series is inspired by his career in healthcare and experience with robotic surgery devices. The travel novels are inspired by his actual vacations in the countries featured in the books.

Prior to writing fiction, he enjoyed a goldilocks career in healthcare, government, and national defense. For ten years, he was a leading robotic surgery researcher, publishing his results in medical journals and speaking at surgical conferences. He spent four years in civilian government service, leading the technology innovation for all US Army simulation systems. Prior to that, he was a vice president for multiple defense software companies.

Dr. Smith has received multiple awards for his innovations in robotic surgery education, training simulation, and software system development. He is on the faculty of the University of Central Florida's College of Medicine and the Institute for Simulation and Training.

He holds a doctorate and MBA from the University of Maryland, a master's from Texas Tech University, and a bachelor's from Colorado State University.

He lives with his wife, dogs, and cats in sunny Florida, frequently escaping to cooler climes during the beastly Florida summers.

STAY IN TOUCH

The Story Never Ends. Join Us:
I always write an epilogue, spinoff, or bonus
adventure to my books. Join our community of
readers to receive all these extras.

www.rddsmith.com/free

ACKNOWLEDGMENTS

As an author, I am infinitely grateful to my readers who invest their time, money, and imaginations in following my stories and characters through their challenges, failures, and transformations.

First, to my wife and children, who have endured decades of fanatic immersion into whatever my latest passion is, most recently, these novels. Your patience, dedication, and love are appreciated every day.

For my introduction and immersion into robotic surgery, I am indebted to Dr. Richard Satava for the professional connections that brought me into this field, for including me in multiple research and educational projects, inviting me to the podium of surgical conferences, co-authoring journal publications, and the years of mentoring that helped me understand the worlds of medicine and surgery. I would like to thank Dr. Vipul Patel, who generously shared his world-class expertise in robotic urology and for the dozens of invitations to observe and learn in his operating room. I am grateful to Dr. Arnold Advincula for leading me into robotic gynecology, including me as a co-director in his robotic fellowship program at Columbia University, and for his friendship and encouragement.

To Rick Wassel, Dr. Monica Reed, Vickie White, and Patrick de la Rosa for entrusting me with the research mission of the AdventHealth Nicholson Center. To the entire staff at the Nicholson Center, especially Alyssa Tanaka and Danielle Julian, who have been invaluable in completing all our research projects. To all the MD surgical fellows whom I had the privilege to lead through their research year: Sanket Chauhan, Mirelle Truong, Kara Simpson, Manuela Perez, Ariel Dubin, Patricia Mattingly, and Jose Luis Mosso Lara. To Tony Nicholson, philanthropist, business leader, and friend.

For my editor Kaitlin Travis, book layout artist Adina Cucicov, and the many advisors who made this book far better than I could have accomplished alone.